THE MARRIAGE SCHEME

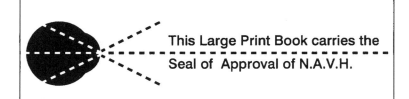

This Large Print Book carries the
Seal of Approval of N.A.V.H.

THE MARRIAGE SCHEME

Patricia K. Azeltine

Thorndike Press • Waterville, Maine

Published in 2002 by arrangement with
Thomas Bouregy & Company, Inc.

Thorndike Press Large Print Candlelight Series.

The tree indicium is a trademark of Thorndike Press.

The text of this Large Print edition is unabridged.
Other aspects of the book may vary from the original edition.

Cover design by Thorndike Press Staff.

Set in 16 pt. Plantin by Minnie B. Raven.

Printed in the United States on permanent paper.

Library of Congress Cataloging-in-Publication Data

Azeltine, Patricia K.
    The marriage scheme / Patricia K. Azeltine.
        p. cm.
    ISBN 0-7862-4097-0 (lg. print : hc : alk. paper)
    1. Inheritance and succession — Fiction.   2. Home
ownership — Fiction.   3. Large type books.   I. Title.
PS3551.A94 M3 2002
813′.6—dc21   2002020033

To my mother, Mary Burian, whose years of encouragement kept me going. You were my inspiration and my best friend. You will remain in my heart and thoughts forever.

Special thanks to my husband Steve and my daughters Mary and Katie. Your love and support mean the world to me!

And thank you Laura Conn for your input and help with this story. You're the best.

Prologue

Beatrice Thompson scratched her head. "I don't know, Dolores. Do you really think this will work?"

"Of course it will. Giving your niece the house and property was a stroke of genius."

"But will Adam take the bait?"

A frown formed on Dolores's thin lips. "He will if I . . . persuade him to."

"You mean nag him."

Dolores rolled her hazel eyes and adjusted her dark brown wig. "I don't nag my son. I merely encourage him."

Bea shook her head. "You nag him but good, especially when it comes to getting married."

Dolores folded her arms over her chest. "I've been waiting thirty-three years for that boy to get married and give me grandbabies to hold and take care of. I'm not going to wait any longer. We'll just have to take the matter into our own hands."

"We?"

Dolores's mouth lifted into a full-fledged smile that emphasized the wrinkles at each corner. "We've been friends for sixty years. Haven't we done almost everything together?" She picked up her coffee and took a sip, then set the dainty china cup back in its saucer.

Bea rubbed her hands together, a nervous gesture she never was able to kick. "But don't you think our actions are a bit drastic? I mean, reminding Adam about the property line. The situation could become scandalous."

"Good. 'Bout time my son did something scandalous when it comes to women. All he cares about is his construction business. Unless a nymph is running around a construction site, my son isn't going to meet a woman when he's out building a road. And I can't think of a better match for my son than your niece, Khara. She's such a sweet girl. Think of this as step one in our Marriage Scheme project."

Bea sighed. Once Dolores put her mind to something there was no changing it. "Very well. You just make sure no one gets hurt."

"We'll make sure of that."

"There's that 'we' again."

Chapter One

Khara Thompson sat nervously at an out-of-the-way table in a small café, dotted with tables for two and four, all covered with red-and-white checkered tablecloths. She hated blind dates. Worse yet, she hated the fact that her aunt had set this one up. She loved her aunt, loved her dearly, and owed her much. It was just that —

Khara's thoughts broke off as a tall, athletically built man wearing jeans and a black-and-red plaid shirt stepped into the café. He moved with smooth coordination and easy grace, and headed right for her. Moisture formed on the palms of her hands and she wiped them on her tan pants, then tugged to straighten her peach blouse before he reached the table. Her heart pounded a little harder when he stopped in front of her, his deep brown eyes boring down at her.

"Are you Khara Thompson?"

She smiled and nodded, suddenly unable to find her voice.

Extending his hand, he said, "I'm Adam

Mansfield." His large, calloused hand enveloped hers.

Once he sat down his stare never wavered from her face and she could tell he was assessing his "date" for the afternoon. The intensity in his dark eyes seemed to bore a hole right through her head, yet she felt an attraction for the man immediately. And what woman wouldn't? He had rugged good looks, with dark brown hair, tan skin, a smooth angle to his cheekbones and jaw, and dark brows that would attract just about any woman over the age of fifteen. Tall, dark, and handsome would be a typical description of him. But there was something else about him, something Khara couldn't quite put her finger on, an indefinable quality that left her uneasy.

This man didn't need to be set up on a date. So why would he have agreed to this meeting?

"Do you always have your aunt set you up on dates?" Adam asked. The rich timbre of his voice was smooth and deep — and commanding.

Khara placed her hands around her coffee cup and felt grateful when the waitress, chewing a wad of gum, interrupted. She handed them menus and poured Adam a cup of hot, steaming coffee.

After the waitress left Adam persisted. "Well? Do you?"

Khara could feel the heat rise in her cheeks. "No." She dipped her head before meeting his penetrating stare again. "I just moved here from Seattle. Aunt Bea was afraid I'd get lonely, so she set this meeting up." She probably should have called it a date but she couldn't bring herself to say the word.

"I would guess my mother had something to do with this."

A lengthy pause fell over the table.

Khara glanced over the menu, searching her mind for something to say. It had been ages since she had dated. Her entire world had been wrapped up in her teaching job, working with children with learning disorders. She hadn't realized until now how it and the children had taken over her life. Perhaps moving to a smaller town in western Washington hadn't been such a bad idea, to live a quiet, peaceful life alone, just like her aunt had.

"I heard that your aunt gave you her house and property."

Khara had a hard time meeting his gaze and shifted in her chair. She hadn't felt right about accepting the gift, but Aunt Bea had insisted, wanting Khara to receive her inheritance before Bea died. All that talk about death and dying had made Khara uncomfortable. Family was important to her, and Bea was the only family she had around. Khara couldn't bear to think of losing her.

"Yes. She did," Khara said in a quiet voice.

"That was very generous of her."

"Yes. It was." She sounded like an idiot, even to herself. Why was she having such a hard time talking to this man? Maybe it was because of the way he seemed to look straight into her very soul, or maybe it was because of his confident manner that bordered on arrogance and left her unsure. Whatever it was, she just wanted this date to be over with. After all, a moving van was coming tomorrow with all her stuff. She had things to do.

Another uncomfortable pause lingered between them. Khara stared blindly at the special of the day, hoping to look too preoccupied to talk.

"Well, I have to admit I wanted to meet you," Adam said. "That's one reason I agreed to this blind date."

Khara drew her brows together and glanced over the menu at him. "And the other reason?"

Adam pulled a piece of paper out of his pocket and handed it to her. His voice suddenly turned serious. "I own the property next to yours. I had a survey done."

She slowly unfolded the paper and stared at a copy of a drawing.

Using a red pencil, Adam had traced the property boundary. "Years ago it was discovered that the original owner had built his home on the property line. I had promised my mother that as long as your aunt was living there I wouldn't do anything about it, but now that you own it I'm letting you know that part of your house is on my land."

Khara could feel the blood drain from her face as his words sank in. She licked her lips, finding them as dry as her mouth. "How could that be?"

Adam lifted his hands, palms up, fingers extended. "The original builder didn't bother to check before he built."

"I can't believe this. I mean . . ." She lifted her shoulders, her eyes wide, her mind whirling. "Did my aunt know about this?"

"She wasn't much for taking care of business matters. She could have contested the boundary when I went to court over it, but she never did."

Suddenly, a thought struck Khara. She stared at Adam, seeing him for the scoundrel he was. "The only reason you came here today was to drop this bombshell on me, wasn't it?" She forced a breath out in disgust and shook her head, not giving him a chance to reply. "You're unbelievable." The legs of her chair screeched across the floor as she pushed back and stood, grabbing her purse.

"I wouldn't leave yet," Adam said. "There's more."

"More?" How could there be more?

"Sit down, please."

"I don't think I want to sit across from you or be anywhere near you." Khara took a step to leave.

Adam's hand shot out and captured her wrist. "Now that's going to be a problem, because I need a place to live while my house is being built. I intend to live in yours."

Khara's jaw dropped. Numbly, she shook her head. "I haven't even moved in yet. You can't . . ."

"I can and I will."

"I'll call the police."

"I grew up here. I know all of them on a first-name basis."

"Then, I'll — I'll see a lawyer."

"Go ahead. But if you don't agree to let me live there I'll make you move your house off of my land."

"Move a house? How am I supposed to do that?" Khara clamped her lips together and lifted her chin to a proud angle as she glared at Adam. Her gaze dipped to his hand, then met his eyes. Slowly, his fingers loosened. Slipping her purse strap over her shoulder, she left the café. The bright sunlight stung her eyes and she squinted as she charged to her white compact car. He wasn't going to have the last word on this if she could help it.

Khara dug in her purse for her keys, unable to find them. She glanced at the person coming out of the café. Great. Adam headed right for her. Where were those keys when she needed them?

He paused right behind her and leaned his back against a black truck parked next to hers.

Khara stiffened, aware of his presence and smelling the rich scent of his after-shave. This man bothered her way too much. She never reacted this strongly to problems. Of course, she'd never encountered one quite this serious before. Level-headed. That's what her father had always called her and that's exactly how she would react to this situation — and Adam Mansfield.

Where were those darn keys?

"Having trouble?" he asked with a hint of humor.

"The only trouble I'm having, Mr. Mansfield, is with you." From the corner of her eye she watched him bend down and pick something up off the gravel.

"Looking for these?" He dangled the key ring from his index finger. When she reached out to take the keys his hand grasped hers. "I need a place to stay. It's only temporary." He had a trace of desperation in his voice, yet no emotion could be seen in his eyes.

Unable to keep a constant stare on him, she looked away. "How do I know I can trust you?"

"Your aunt and my mother are best friends, and have been for years. I wouldn't try anything. Do you really think I'm the type of man who would hurt a woman?"

She forced a breath out in disgust and glared at him. "All I know is that you're the type of man who would blackmail a woman."

He dipped his chin, unable to meet her eyes for several long seconds. When he looked at her the intensity had returned,

16

no apology, no regret. "Sometimes we're forced to do things that are unpleasant."

"Does your mother know you're doing this?"

Adam laughed, a genuine smile curved his lips. "My mother would scream with joy if she thought I was 'settling down' with a woman."

She jerked her hand free. "We'll see about that." Khara turned back to her car. Hoping her hand wouldn't shake, she jammed the key in the door and unlocked it.

"You're not in Seattle anymore, Khara. You don't need to lock your doors."

She wished he would stop standing so close to her. He disturbed her concentration, or was his spicy aftershave doing that? Opening the door, she tossed her purse inside, then pivoted to face him. "It's Ms. Thompson to you, and I think I'd be safer locking my doors even if I am in a small town." She turned around and sat down in the car.

Adam shut her door and watched her back out of the parking lot and drive away. He hadn't expected her to be so beautiful. He liked how the fire danced in her green eyes when she got angry — and the curve of her mouth, so full, so delicate, so tempting. Her thick, dark auburn hair framed her angelic face, and glittered flecks of gold and red in the sunlight. He wondered if the strands were as silky as they looked.

He continued to stare down the street from which she had long ago disappeared. He couldn't remember ever reacting to a woman the way he had the moment he'd seen Khara, sitting there in the café, nervously licking her lips and holding her hands to keep them from shaking. It didn't take a genius to figure out she didn't date very often. If she had, some guy would have snatched her up long ago.

He stepped over to his truck and opened the door. Though he set his key in the ignition, he didn't turn it on. Instead he rested his hands on the base of the wheel. He could still feel the adrenaline coursing through his veins. Normally the adrenaline would have come from a business deal that had gone well, but the emotion that pumped through him right now had nothing to do with business.

For years he'd heard Bea talk about Khara. He felt as if he knew her. He'd even seen pictures of her. High school pictures, that is. No doubt about it. She had blossomed into one beautiful woman. Khara reminded him a lot of Bea. Quiet and calm, but with an underlying strength, that kind of strength a man needed from a woman, that *he* needed from a woman.

He shook his head. His mother would just love to hear his thoughts right now, but he wouldn't give her that satisfaction. He would share living space with Khara, nothing more. No woman had gotten to him yet, at least not since his college days, long ago, and he didn't intend for one to get to him now. He would keep his distance from Khara, focus on his work, his company — and the *real* reason he needed to stay at her house, to find out who'd been stealing and sabotaging his business. It would be better that way. Women complicated a man's life. And he refused to let another one trample his heart.

Khara knocked on Bea's door and tapped her foot while she waited. The second it opened she pushed her way in. The wrinkles on Bea's forehead deepened. "What's wrong, dear?"

"Adam Mansfield. That's what's wrong."

Bea and Dolores exchanged worried glances. "What did my son do?" Dolores asked with concern.

Khara paced across the living room, her

arms folded over her chest, her heart thudding. "He's moving in my house and he says I don't have a choice." She drummed her fingers on her opposite arm. "If he thinks I am going to sit by and let him move in without a fight, he's dead wrong."

"He does need a place to live," Bea said.

"Shortly before you moved here a windstorm smashed a tree through his house. It was left in shambles. Until his log cabin is built he has nowhere to live," Dolores explained.

Khara vaguely heard the ladies' words, her mind still a whirl from the news Adam had dropped on her. "He said that part of the house you gave me is on *his* property and if I don't let him stay there he'll make me move it." She lifted her hands in the air. "How do you move a house? The man is being unreasonable." Khara looked at her aunt. "Did you know about this?"

Bea rubbed her hands together. "How about if I make us some tea?" She stepped into the kitchen.

"Of all the nerve," Khara said and paced back across the room. "Can't he rent an apartment or get a motel room? Why my house?"

"Because it's next door to the log home he's having built. And it's located near the mountains where he works," Dolores said.

"Lucky me."

"It won't be that bad. In fact, I bet you'll hardly notice he's there at all. His business keeps him so busy, he'll probably be gone most of the time." Age and time had shortened Dolores's tall, wiry body so that she was slightly hunched at the shoulders. When she narrowed her stare and puckered her lips, the wrinkles around her eyes, mouth, and chin deepened. Dolores's eyes were filled with worry. And something else. Perhaps irritation.

"You think so?" Khara asked.

Dolores smiled and displayed her bleached white false teeth. "I'm sure of it. Now come over here, sit down at the table, and have a cup of tea and freshly baked oatmeal cookies. Once you calm down you'll see that all this fussing is for nothing."

"I'll have to take a rain check on the tea and cookies." Khara stepped to the door. "There's something I have to do first. Tell Aunt Bea that I'll talk to her later." Before Dolores could object, Khara whipped open the door and stepped through, shutting it behind her. She hurried to her car, revved the engine, and drove until she reached the first phone booth she came to. On the property drawing Adam had shown her, she remembered seeing Acme Surveying. She searched through the phone book and wrote down the address and phone number, then sought out the company in town.

Inside the building was a multitude of offices of various small businesses. Finding ACME SURVEYING on a door, she knocked. A deep voice said, "Come in."

Khara found her pulse beat a little faster as she stepped inside the cramped quarters. She read the name plate FRED NEWMAN on the cluttered desk as he punched away at the computer in front of him. "Mr. Newman, I need to talk to you about a survey you did that adjoins my property."

He held his finger up for her to wait a moment.

Khara glanced around the small room. In one corner a metal tripod and wood stakes leaned against the wall. One table was filled with rolls of colorful tape, an instrument, and stacks of drawings scattered about, some rolled up and others spread out. A pot of freshly brewed coffee filled the air with a strong aroma but it couldn't hide the musty scent in the room.

He turned his attention to her, stood, and extended his hand. "You must be Ms. Thompson."

"How do you know my name?" Khara asked in surprise.

"Adam called me and said you might be stopping by." Fred Newman turned to the table behind him and searched through several drawings, his tanned skin indicating the long hours he'd spent working outdoors. "Here it is." He laid out a large paper that had the house, driveway, three acres, and property line drawn on it. "I have to tell you that this is a rare case, but it can happen."

"So you are saying the property line does run through my house?"

A sympathetic expression deepened his deep-set blue eyes and accentuated his graying brows. "I'm afraid so."

"Why can't I buy the land my house sits on?"

He tilted his head; a few strands of hair slid to one side and uncovered his receding hairline. "You can if the owner of the land is willing to sell. If he isn't, then your only other choice is to move your house."

She folded her arms over her chest. "How am I supposed to move a house?"

He raised his eyebrows. "There are companies that do that, but it'll cost you."

Dread knotted Khara's stomach. She had very little money, and what savings she did have had to last her until she could find a full-time teaching position. Luckily Bea was able to help her find a few private tutoring jobs, but that would only last until school started. The way things were shaping up, this would be one long summer.

"What if I take it to court?"

"Adam's already done that. Your aunt never disputed it. In fact she never showed up."

"Was she notified?" Khara drew in a deep breath to calm her nerves. Nothing seemed to help.

"Sure. She got papers on it."

"My aunt is seventy years old. Her husband always took care of these matters for her. Since his death she wouldn't have known what to do. She probably didn't even understand what the letter said."

Fred Newman shrugged. "The only other thing you can do is find a good lawyer that specializes in land disputes in the state of Washington and take it to court again. You could claim adverse possession." He rubbed the bristles on his face, making a chafing sound. "Since you're a new owner you might have a case. It's hard to say."

Khara knew she had just lost. Hire a lawyer? He might as well have told her to buy the Taj Mahal. She couldn't afford a lawyer. She tried to smile but one never formed.

"Funny thing how property brings out the worst in people, isn't it?" Fred said.

Hilarious, she thought sarcastically. "Thanks for your time."

He rolled the paper up and handed it to her. "You keep this." As she turned to leave he added, "You might think about tearing down the family room and rebuilding it on the other side. That's the part of the house that's on the wrong side of the property line. 'Course, half of your kitchen hangs over the line too." He shook his head. "Sorry I couldn't give you better news."

A lump filled her throat. She couldn't have replied if she had wanted to. So she nodded, then left. By the time she reached the car her hand had fisted around the drawing, crumpling it in the middle. She tossed it in the backseat. Her mind whirled with possible solutions to her problem, but the real problem was that Adam Mansfield had control over this situation. He owned the land that half of her house sat on and he had the power to make her move it. For now she didn't have a choice. She would have to let Adam move in whether she liked it or not.

Chapter Two

Khara drove down a long dirt driveway and vowed to fill every pothole with gravel as soon as possible. Tall green grass grew on both sides of the drive until the road ended at the front of the house. For a moment she just sat in the car and stared at the white building with its chipped and peeled paint from years of neglect. The windows were dirty and the roof looked in dire need of repair. Dandelions flourished in the flower garden that lined the front of the house on both sides of the covered porch.

Taking a deep breath, she reached for the drawing in the backseat, got out of the car, and shut the door. An eagle screeched a greeting to her as it flew high above and landed in a thick grove of fir trees that grew so high they looked as if they were in a race to reach the sun. Brilliant white puffy clouds contrasted with a deep blue sky. The smell of wild roses filled the air and Khara closed her eyes as she breathed in the sweet scent. Most of the three acres she now owned was pasture, but thick woods surrounded her property on three sides, giving her the privacy she desired.

She knew that Aunt Bea hadn't lived here for several years, but Khara had no idea it was in such bad shape. Hopefully, it was a little better on the inside. As soon as she opened the front door a musty, dusty odor attacked her nose, making her cough. Going straight to the windows, she opened them and the curtains. A gentle breeze immediately refreshed the room. Today, she would scrub the house free of years of dust.

The tension in Khara's shoulder and neck began to ease just as the phone rang. When she heard Adam's voice on the other end a knot formed in the pit of her stomach.

"I just wanted to let you know that I'll be moving my stuff in tomorrow."

"I can't wait," Khara said in a deadpan voice.

He hesitated before he said, "I really appreciate you letting me stay there."

"Like I have a choice?"

"Yeah, well. I think everything will work out just fine. See you tomorrow." Click.

Khara plopped the phone in its cradle. It really wasn't the fact that Adam was moving in that made her so mad. It was the way he went about it. If he'd just asked if he could stay with her for a while, she probably would have said yes. After all, he was her aunt's best friend's son. It wasn't uncommon for her to help others. But Adam hadn't given her a choice. He'd resorted to threats.

She didn't intend to make it easy for him because of that.

A roll of masking tape rested on the kitchen counter and she scooted it aside to lay the drawing out. Her glance flew back to the masking tape. *That's it!* she thought triumphantly. She picked up the tape and grabbed a chair. Using her best judgment of where the line ran through the house, she started at the ceiling and ran the tape down the wall, over the center of the stove, across the floor, over the island counter, across more of the floor and back up the opposite wall. There. Close enough. Adam would not be allowed to cross that line. He could live in the portion of the house that was on his property. Nothing more.

By mid-afternoon the sky had turned gray. Khara followed the moving van to her new home. She immediately noticed a black pickup truck parked in the driveway. When she turned the knob on the front door she found it unlocked. Her eyes widened, finding the living room fully furnished.

A forest green and gold comforter covered a large bed in the master bedroom. A cherrywood dresser and nightstand were placed beside it. The bathroom had men's toiletry items, and in the closet were men's clothes.

Of all the nerve!

"Where do you want this, lady?" one of the movers hollered from the foyer.

Khara came out of the bedroom as he set his end of the couch down, an impatient expression on his bristled face. "Just a minute. I'll be right back." She crossed the house and entered the kitchen, then family room. There she found Adam setting up a large-screen television and VCR. He glanced over his shoulder before returning his undivided attention back to the wires.

"What do you think you're doing?"

"I'm connecting my television and VCR."

She placed her hands on her hips and expelled a sigh of frustration. "You know what I mean. Why is your furniture in my house?"

He looked back to her, his brows together. "I told you I was moving in, remember? I thought you might need furniture to fill the house, so I used mine."

"Why would you think I need furniture?" She looked at him as if he were insane and folded her arms over her chest.

Adam stood, then lifted his shoulders and grimaced at the same time. "Judging by your car —"

"What's wrong with my car?"

"It's not exactly a Mercedes. Why are you getting so mad about this?"

She tilted her head slightly back to meet him in the eyes, and noticed how his dark brown eyes almost looked black. "This is my house and I want your things out of my bedroom and living room so I can put *my* furniture in there."

He lifted his hands in surrender. "Fine. I was just trying to help out. I'll move my stuff into the garage."

"One side of the garage," she added. "I want to be able to park my car in it." Khara followed Adam into the living room and noticed the elegance of his furniture. The tan sofa and love seat complemented the paneled wall much better than the floral mauve print of her couch. For a fleeting second she contemplated keeping his things in the house and moving hers out to the garage, but she quickly dismissed the idea. This was her house, and nice or not, she would decorate it with her belongings until she could afford to get something new.

Adam climbed in his truck and departed after he'd moved his furniture into the garage. When the movers finished up and sped away, Khara spent the rest of the afternoon unpacking boxes. She couldn't seem to shake the notion that Adam just assumed she would prefer his furniture to her own. Another thing that bothered her was how easily he'd turned the tables on her, saying he was trying to help her by moving his stuff in and automatically claiming the big bedroom. The only person he was trying to help was himself.

To calm her frayed nerves, Khara did what relaxed her most. She cooked. Of course, a generous swig of cooking sherry would have helped to ease the tension in her muscles, she thought with a grin. Every time she cooked or baked she thought of Joel. They had met when she was going to college and he was studying to become a chef. He taught her many things in the kitchen. Unfortunately, their relationship never got as heated as their flambé did. She would have married Joel if he'd asked her, but she quickly learned that he had loved her like a sister, and nothing more. He left her with a broken heart and skills that would rival any cook, man or woman. When Khara looked back on it, she realized they had nothing in common except for their love of cooking.

After several hours Khara had a feast fit for a king — and no one to eat it besides her. The kitchen door opened. In walked Adam carrying a large box. He set his load down on the floor and dragged in a deep breath. "What smells so good? Are we expecting company?"

"No, *we* aren't expecting anyone. I cook when I'm upset; it relaxes me. Now that you're moved in I'm surprised I don't have an entire smorgasbord whipped up."

Adam grinned. "If it tastes as good as it smells I think I'm going to have to keep you upset the entire time I'm here."

"I'm sure just your presence will do that."

His grin never faltered until his gaze followed the path of the tape as if seeing it for the first time. "Don't tell me, you're using that masking tape to hold the house together."

Khara bit back a laugh.

Trying to sound angry she said, "I'm so glad you brought that up, Mr. Mansfield. I meant to tell you this earlier, but you disappeared before I got a chance to. The tape indicates where the property line runs through my house. Which means that you can only occupy the portion of the house that's on your land." She could tell he wasn't sure whether to take her seriously or not. "If you cross this line you'll be trespassing."

Adam carried his box into the family room, and moments later returned to the kitchen, set a pan on the stove, and placed a box of macaroni and cheese on the counter. From the corner of her eye she watched him read the box instructions, then glance at the sink, which was located on *her* side of the house.

"I need water," Adam said.

"The hose is outside the kitchen door."

He forced a breath out his nose. Khara could feel his eyes boring a hole on the side of her head, but she refused to look at him. Moments later, the back door whipped open. The second Adam left the room she let a giggle escape and tried her best to quickly wipe the smile away when he stepped back inside. He dumped the noodles in the water and turned the burner on high.

"You should let the water boil first before you add the noodles," Khara said, her back still to him.

"I don't cook too often."

"Oh? I couldn't tell." A grin spread on her lips as she glanced over her shoulder at him.

"Can I have a spoon to stir the noodles?"

She ripped the lettuce leaf in her hand and dropped it in the salad bowl. Without looking at him she said, "Is it on your side of the line?"

"No."

"Then what do you think?"

Several long seconds of quiet lingered. "I think this is going to be one long summer." Stepping from the kitchen, he entered the family room and returned with a small spoon in hand.

Khara moved to the stove and opened the oven to check on her homemade biscuits.

"Sure smells good," Adam said.

Khara could almost see him salivating. Just as she reached to stir the gravy Adam's hand extended out to his noodles and their fingers touched. Their eyes met and held for several long seconds, then Khara quickly glanced away. "You first," she said, hoping he didn't notice the level of disturbance in her voice.

"No, you go ahead. It wouldn't matter if I ruined my noodles." He inhaled deeply. "That gravy smells good. I'd hate to see you burn it." He gestured with a wave of his hand. As she stirred he said, "Yes, sir, that gravy smells good. You going to eat it all by yourself?"

"Are you giving me a hint you want to eat my dinner instead of yours?"

"Yep. That's exactly what I'm doing. So how about it?"

Khara rolled her eyes. Why was it that all men ever thought about was their stomach? She gazed into his pleading brown eyes and felt her heart soften. "I should dump the dinner on your head, especially since you tried to steal the master bedroom."

The corners of his mouth turned upward. "And waste all that good food?" As if the matter was settled, Adam shut the burner off and went out the back door. When he returned he carried another box into "his" portion of the house. "I just realized there's no bedroom in here."

Khara stepped over to the opening between the kitchen and the family room. With the wooden spoon in her hand she pointed. "The couch folds out to a bed and you have a bathroom with a shower stall." She intended to hold her ground on the matter. This man forced his way into her home and into her life. Now he would have to live by *her* rules.

Adam didn't take long to haul in a few more boxes, and by the time Khara had set dishes and silverware on the island counter, and dished up dinner, he had washed up and sat on a stool. He spent little time talking until he had eaten one full plate and had started on another. "You are one good cook. Is that what you do for a living?"

"No. I'm a teacher."

"That's right. Your aunt told me that." He stared at her, a strange expression in his eyes. Perhaps he wondered if there was any dessert?

Khara's heart beat a little faster. "Why are you looking at me that way?"

"I'm just wondering how such a beautiful woman could be so talented in so many areas."

Khara had heard that line before, usually from men that wanted much more than she was willing to give. But this time it didn't sound like a line. In her mind was the image of Adam's strong arms around her, his muscular chest pressed against her, his lips caressing hers . . . what was she thinking!

"Are you blushing at my compliment?" Adam asked.

Khara felt her whole face flame hot. She got off her stool and placed her plate in the sink. "Yes, that's it." Her reply sounded lame. She knew it and she could tell Adam did too. She filled the sink and began to wash the dishes, hoping he would drop the subject.

Minutes later Adam got off his stool and walked over to her. "That's the best meal I've ever had."

"You ate enough for ten people." She tried to sound stern, but couldn't.

"I tend to take advantage of opportunities." Standing only inches behind her, he reached out and placed his plate on the counter beside the sink. His breath stirred strands of her hair and lightly touched her neck, sending shivers down her spine.

Khara hated her reaction to him. She wanted to hate this man. She did hate this man. But her actual reaction to him was hard to ignore. A man in her life wouldn't work. She was independent, self-sufficient, had a career she loved, and led a comfortable life. As soon as the thought entered her mind she knew it was a lie. No, she led a boring life, at least socially.

A tingling spread from the pit of her

stomach out to her limbs. Khara knew she wasn't acting or reacting like herself around Adam. Keeping her distance, she could remain in command around men, but Adam seemed to zap every ounce of control she had. She didn't need the heart-aches that always accompanied a relation-ship. In the end the man would only leave her. Everyone else had, either through death or distance. Inevitably it would happen. She couldn't take the pain, the loss. Not again.

His voice was near her ear when he said, "I have a proposition for you."

She held her breath. Her heart pounded. As he stepped away, the heat of his body was replaced by cold air. A sense of disap-pointment fluttered through her. With soapy hands she turned around and formed the best scowl she could. "Proposi-tion?"

One corner of his mouth lifted in a lop-sided grin and he leaned his hip against the counter. He scanned her face. "Yes, a proposition."

She placed a fist on her hip. "And what does this proposition entail?"

"I want to hire you to cook and clean for me during the time I live here. I'll pay you well for your services."

A flash of alarm pierced her mind. She hoped he couldn't see the attraction she felt for him, especially if it wasn't reciprocated. At the moment she couldn't tell if he was toying with her or was truly interested. A part of her didn't want to know. With the way Adam barged into her life, it would be best for her to keep him at a distance. Safer. Her whole life she'd played it safe. Now wasn't the time to be reckless.

She should be angry with him, lashing out, not making him dinner. Her mind was muddled. She had been alone for so long she acted desperate for companionship, for love. That had to be why she was reacting to Adam the way she was. It just had to be.

"I'll cook your meals and wash your clothes, but you have to make your bed, pick up the family room, and help with dishes. Is it a deal?"

He nodded. "Fair enough. I'm sure you're going to need that extra money."

"Why?"

"In order to move this house."

Suddenly, Khara's heart went stone cold and her body stiffened. The reminder of what Adam intended to do broke the moment — and any attraction she felt for him. With clenched teeth she said, "How could I forget?" Turning around, she busied herself with the dishes. Every muscle in her shoulders tightened until they ached.

After Adam walked out of the kitchen, Khara glanced over her shoulder into the family room and spotted him unpacking, his back to her. Somehow, some way, she intended to get this man out of her house. She didn't care if he was the son of her aunt's best friend. She didn't care if he had nowhere to go, no place to live. His problems were no concern of hers. And she intended to keep it that way.

Chapter Three

After a restless night's sleep Khara woke up to the sound of big engines roaring and brakes squealing. She glanced at the clock and groaned. Seven in the morning. This was the first summer in years she didn't have to fill her days and nights taking college courses and studying. All school year long she had looked forward to sleeping in, at least until eight or nine. She rolled out of bed, slipped her pink fluffy slippers on, wrapped up in her thick, pastel-green terrycloth bathrobe, and walked out to the kitchen.

Just as she reached the counter two men rushed in the door without knocking, gave her strange looks, and hastened into the family room. Khara's glance followed them, then her eyes widened. Adam had set up an office smack in the middle of the family room. He had the phone, *her* phone, stretched from the kitchen and placed on a large wooden desk. He sat in a leather chair behind it. Several file cabinets lined one wall. Adam's glance met Khara's for a second.

"Khara," Adam said, "would you make us a pot of coffee?"

An irritation ignited inside her. What was she, his secretary now? This man's nerve had no bounds. Rather than argue the matter in front of two strangers, she bit her tongue and filled the coffeepot with water. She would make coffee only because she needed a cup of hot, rich brew to wake her up. She heard another loud roar of an engine. While the coffee percolated she went into the living room and looked out her front window. Her eyes widened. Parked in her driveway was two large trucks, a grader, huge dozer, and a hauling truck with a loader on it. Her yard looked more like a dealership for big equipment than a residence. Feeling a headache coming on, she rubbed her forehead and temples.

She returned to her bedroom, showered, and dressed. After she brushed her hair out, she entered the kitchen. Adam sat alone at his desk, sipping a cup of coffee.

"What exactly is going on?" she asked. "Why does my front yard look like a used bulldozer lot? And why are strange men running in and out of my house?"

Adam scribbled something down and seconds later looked up. "I run my business out of my home. Now that I'm living here, I'll be running it from here."

No doubt about it, the man had lost his mind. "Are you crazy? This is *my* home, and you've just turned it into a circus. I won't allow this."

He leaned back in his chair, undaunted by her statement. "You agreed to let me live here."

She forced a breath out. "Like I had a choice."

He shrugged. "Nevertheless, we have an agreement. Where I live is where I work."

She stepped over the taped line and into the family room, her hands on her hips. Heat rose in her cheeks from burning anger. "You're not going to work in my house."

"Normally it's not this busy. Today's kind of hectic." He pushed out of his chair, came around the desk, and stood a few feet in front of her, his arms folded over his chest.

"I don't care. I want you, your men, and your big machines off of my property, now."

His thick brows drew together and in a mocking tone he said, "*Whose* property?"

Khara's chest rose and fell with each breath. She grabbed an empty box and placed it on his desk, then filled it with his papers. "If you won't pack up and leave, then I'll do it for you."

In a calm, relaxed manner he watched her. "So you must be planning on moving your house off of my land today."

Her hands froze. She stared at the contents in the box for several seconds before she met his gaze, a hard gleam in his eyes as if daring her to challenge him. A lump of frustration formed in her throat. He enjoyed having the upper hand over her. She could tell. Khara fought back the tears of frustration that threatened to blur her vision. Her nostrils flared with each intake of air.

Masking any emotion, Adam said, "Why don't you go make breakfast?"

She stepped in front of him, her hands fisted at her side. "You can make your own breakfast." As she started to walk away he grabbed her arm.

"You sure make it a habit of breaking agreements, don't you?" When she wouldn't reply he added, "I hired you to cook and clean for me, remember? You agreed to it. I expect you to hold up your end."

Her glare turned into a sneer. "You know what I intend to do with the money I

44

make from you? I intend to hire an attorney to fight this land dispute, and get you out of my home and out of my life." She jerked her arm free.

Adam studied her, a grin lifting the corners of his mouth, a frown wrinkling his forehead, drawing his brows together. "Are you always this cranky in the morning?"

Something between a scream and growl ripped from her throat before she walked away. His chair creaked as he sat down. She swore he chuckled. Khara felt like burning his breakfast, but she couldn't do that to good food. It went against her beliefs to waste food when she saw so many children who had so little.

In just thirty minutes she whipped up scrambled eggs, bacon, sausage, toast, a glass of orange juice, and a mug of coffee. She placed the plate on the lunch counter with a clank and said, "Breakfast is served, Master."

Her sarcasm didn't go unnoticed. Instead of angering him, he laughed. His smile never wavered until he sat down. "Aren't you joining me?"

She tilted her head. "Is that a requirement of the job?"

"No, but . . ."

"But what?"

He hesitated before he said, "Nothing."

For a moment she watched him gulp the food down as if he hadn't eaten in weeks. A slight satisfaction cooled her temper, knowing he really appreciated her cooking. He didn't have to say anything. His actions spoke louder than words. "I have an appointment at ten o'clock this morning. Try to be out of here by then." Pivoting, she stalked out of the room. She could feel his eyes on her until she turned the corner into her bedroom.

Taylor Jenks arrived right on time for his first lesson. His mother dropped him off and said she would return two hours later. Khara wondered if his mother really cared about Taylor's problem or if she just wanted to get rid of him for a couple hours. Whatever her reasons were, it didn't matter. Khara would be able to work with the boy all summer long.

"You can call me Teacher Khara." Khara spoke and, using her hands, signed at the same time.

The little boy signed back. "You can call me Taylor."

A smile creased her lips. She already liked Taylor. He was a nice relief after having to deal with Adam. And much more quiet.

Khara had already talked by phone to Taylor's preschool teachers and read the test results, evaluation, and recommendations specialists had made. On top of having a difficult time speaking, Taylor also had dyslexia, seeing letters and words backward. By the end of summer Khara hoped to have Taylor identifying his numbers and the alphabet.

Taking him by the hand, she led him into the kitchen, and lifted him onto the stool Adam seemed to have claimed as his own. His bright red curly hair matched the five-year-old's happy disposition. They talked for a while so he could become comfortable with her, then slowly eased into a lesson. The lesson had no more begun when hammering pounded on the roof. Khara rubbed her forehead. Since Adam had moved in, less than twenty-four hours ago, a constant headache lingered just below the surface. She got Taylor started on an assignment, then went to investigate the noise.

Parked out front was a truck that read, *Mike's Roofing Company. Fast and Reliable.* Khara couldn't believe what she was seeing or hearing. How could one man disrupt her life so completely, so thoroughly? She scanned the yard and spotted Adam working on the engine of one of the trucks. She charged over to him and cleared her throat.

Adam had his head buried under the open hood. He grunted on an exhale before he lifted his head and reached for a wrench that sat on the edge of the truck. A momentary look of surprise flashed in and out of his eyes as if he'd never heard her. He returned his attention to the engine and seemed deeply absorbed in it when he said, "Don't tell me, lunch is ready."

"Is that all you ever think about? I want to know why there's a roofer on my house."

Adam didn't reply until after he'd tightened a bolt. "Funny thing happened last night after I lay down to sleep. A leak dripped water on my forehead. I had to move the foldout couch three times." He straightened to a standing position, wiped his greasy hands on a rag, and met her gaze at the last second. "You wouldn't happen to know anything about that, would you?"

She opened her mouth to speak, then closed it and glanced away. Her aunt had warned her about the leak, but she'd been so angry, she'd neglected to tell him. Last night, she'd giggled when she'd heard him moving the furniture and cursing.

"I didn't think so," Adam said sarcastically.

Her head darted back to him. "I can't conduct my lesson with all that pounding going on. I need quiet so I can concentrate."

"Mike said he'd have the job done today." He tilted his head to one side. " 'Course if he can't finish the job today because you won't let him, then I won't be able to sleep another night and I'll have to bring some of my men in from the field to help with the office work. They could be running in and out of your house all day long." He lifted his shoulders. "I guess it's your choice."

This man could stir her anger up in seconds flat. "You're impossible." Khara didn't want to hear any more. Adam intended to get his way whether she liked it or not. She shook her head and walked away. When she returned to the house she moved Taylor into the living room, set their papers and learning tools on the coffee table, and sat on the floor with him. The hammering was still audible, but they managed to get work done anyway.

Adam stuck his head back under the hood, but his mind wasn't on replacing the spark plugs. All he could think about since he'd arrived was Khara. In the small, cramped house he couldn't concentrate on putting together a bid for timber so he'd decided to go outside and tune up the truck. After all, it needed it. Yet even outside she drifted into his thoughts. It seemed there was no escaping her. Maybe he should chop wood, or run the dozer, grader, or drive a dump truck, anything to get his mind off of her.

Every time he closed his eyes, there she was, with her sparkling green eyes and her lips slightly parted. Heck, it hadn't been the water drops that had kept him awake last night. It had been the thought of her being only a few feet down the hall. All night he thought about her.

He liked the way she lifted her chin in defiance each time she got angry with him. For a moment last night, over dinner, he had seen a softness in her eyes, a softness that drew him to her like a fly to a spider's web. She stirred emotions in him, emotions he had difficulty recognizing. It was more than physical attraction. That he could deal with and knew how to handle. With Khara it was more than that, deeper, something he couldn't put his finger on, something he'd never felt before.

The way she kept her distance with him, he could tell someone had hurt her. Pain was evident in her eyes. He knew her parents had decided to travel the country, rarely contacting her and leaving her alone, but Adam suspected it was more than that. Another man, undoubtedly. He wondered who it was, and why any man could have hurt her.

She was so beautiful. He liked the way her eyes gleamed through her thick lashes and the way her lips pouted when she got annoyed. Most of all, he liked the way she reacted to him. She might hate him now, but there was a fine line between love and hate, one that could easily be crossed, just like the tape down the middle of her kitchen.

An hour later Adam entered the house and washed his hands in the bathroom. As he stepped out, he could hear Khara talking softly to the little boy. He walked quietly to the doorway that led from the kitchen into the living room, leaned his shoulder against the frame, and watched. She had her back to him and was signing words that she spoke out loud.

Adam wasn't sure just how long he stood there watching her, unable to turn his eyes away. He hadn't intended to watch at all, but the tones of her gentle voice, the caring behind each word, drew him in there. She laughed, a low, rippling sound that had a way of softening a man's heart. Just the sight of her sitting there with that child, her heartfelt concern displayed so openly, sent an ache rushing to his heart. A man needed a woman's tenderness like that, whether it be in a kiss, a kind word, or a gentle touch.

As if she felt his presence Khara glanced over her shoulder. He'd been caught staring. A flicker of alarm flashed through his gut, then he quickly recovered.

"What can I do for you, Mr. Mansfield?"

"I, uh, was just wondering when lunch would be ready."

"I should have guessed. I'll make lunch when Taylor and I are finished here." She glanced at her watch. "In about forty minutes." She turned back around and continued with her lesson.

Adam pushed away from the wall and wandered back to his desk. He stared at the bid documents and forced himself to concentrate on the words.

Khara placed Adam's clothes in the wash. She couldn't believe anyone could get their jeans as dirty as he did, but she guessed it went with the job, working out-doors in all kinds of weather, building roads. As she lowered the lid and pulled the knob up to start it, she heard a loud boom outside.

"What now?" she muttered to herself and went outside to check on the noise. A huge, empty dump truck had backed into her shed, collapsing it. Khara closed her eyes. Why couldn't she wake up and have this all be a dream?

"It looks like we had an accident," Adam said, coming over to her and standing only a few feet away. "I'll repair it."

"Why don't you go one better and move out?" Khara folded her arms over her chest. She was a simple person with simple needs. This man sure loved to complicate her way of living.

"But then your life would be so boring," he said.

"I like boring. I also like peace and quiet. That's one reason why I moved here."

He gazed at her face as if memorizing every detail. "I can't imagine a beautiful woman like you having a boring life. I bet you left many broken hearts in Seattle."

Khara laughed. "Only five-year-old broken hearts."

His stare settled on his lips before it moved to her eyes. "I find that hard to believe."

"And I think you're trying to sweet talk me out of being angry at you because one of your men destroyed my shed." Khara followed Adam's gaze to the shed, its remains in slabs on the ground. Thankfully she hadn't put anything in it yet. Since she'd had an apartment in Seattle she hadn't collected any yard and gardening tools.

He looked back at her and smiled, that easy smile that was becoming familiar, along with his scent, a woodsy, evergreen smell that she found appealing. Too appealing. For the first time she noticed flecks of gold in his eyes that accented their rich brown. A thin scar, small and white, snaked at the base of his chin. She hadn't noticed it until now, just as she hadn't noticed the depth of his strength, formed in bulging biceps and displayed in his short-sleeved shirt.

"Is it working?" he asked.

"No."

His hand stroked his chin, making a chafing sound, his skin a bit rough from lack of a razor that morning. A dump truck made an ear-piercing beeping sound as it unloaded gravel, creeping forward up the driveway. Adam's stare followed the noise.

"What's this?" Khara's hands moved to her hips.

"I'm laying gravel down for the driveway to get rid of the potholes that we graded out." His lips curved slowly, hesitantly.

"Did you ever think of asking me first? I do own this place."

He wagged his finger in the air. "*Part* of this place. Technically your shed was also on my property, but I'll rebuild it on your side of the line."

"And I suppose you expect me to be grateful for that."

A gentle smile touched his lips. "Gratitude would be nice." He raised his brows.

She narrowed her glare at him. She had never met a man that could get her so riled so quickly. Alone. It was what she wanted and how she'd decide her life would be. Living with Adam had never been in her plans, and never would be. She had long ago stopped dreaming about marriage and being with a man, feeling his arms wrapped around her, or giving her a tender, reassuring kiss.

Before she said something stupid she pivoted on her heels. As she walked away she counted to ten.

"I'll take a rain check on that gratitude," Adam said, laughter in his voice.

Khara halted and whirled around, noticing he'd hooked his thumbs in his pockets. "Just see to it you rebuild my shed." She tried to sound forceful, but with the way Adam exuded confidence and control she doubted she could intimidate him in the least.

She charged into the house, shut the door, and entered the kitchen. Today she would bake bread, and she could pretend Adam's neck was the dough. After an hour she set the dough to rise, then turned the oven on. She opened the door and waited for it to heat, but it never did.

Khara inhaled a slow, deep breath. It seemed as if every time she blinked something broke down in this house. Living in an apartment had never been this difficult. She didn't have a clue what to do other than check to make sure the cord was plugged in, which was in back of the stove. She grasped one side of the stove and pulled. It wouldn't budge. She tried again, groaning.

The back door flew open and Adam stepped in. He observed her for a moment before he asked, "You need help?"

"I don't need anything from you, thank you."

"The stove broken?"

"No, I move it for exercise," she said sarcastically.

He folded his arms over his chest, leaned his hip against the counter, and watched. "Just trying to help."

"Well, don't." She expelled another groan as she tried jerking it. The heavy stove moved an inch. Finally she made progress. She glanced over at Adam, the grin on his face irritating her. "Do you have to stand there and stare?"

He raised his hands in the air, then slapped them to his sides. "Fine. If you need help, you know where I'll be."

Khara waited for him to leave before she grabbed the stove and struggled to move it again. It wouldn't budge and she felt like crying. She glanced toward the family room and shook her head. Darn it, she wanted to do this on her own. In rapid succession, she pulled several times, but the stove barely rocked. Dragging in a breath, she expelled a sharp sigh. She didn't have a choice. She'd have to ask Adam for help or her bread would be ruined.

She stepped over to the opening between the kitchen and family room, folded her arms, and said, "Would you help me?"

He cupped his hand behind his ear as if

he had a hard time hearing her. "Did I hear a please?"

"Please." She forced the word out.

A wide smile creased his lips. "Much better. Now what did you want me to help you with?"

"You know I can't move the stove."

He raised his brows, delighting in taunting her. "Oh, yes. The stove." He pushed out of his chair and stepped by her. The muscles in his arms bulged as he gripped the appliance on both sides and lifted it out. Adam brushed his hands together as if it had been as light as a feather. "There you go. Would you like me to see if I can fix it?"

"No!"

He shrugged and went back to his desk.

Khara bit her lower lip. The second the word flew out of her mouth she knew she had made a big mistake. She checked the cord. It was plugged in. Okay, now what? Wires seemed to come and go everywhere. All she could do was stare at them. She didn't have a clue what she was even looking at. The stove was so old she doubted it had a manual. Even if there was one, she knew it wouldn't make any sense to her. She might be able to cook, but fixing the equipment she cooked with wasn't her forte.

She stepped back to the opening and stood there, her arms folded over her chest. She waited for Adam to look up, but he wouldn't. She knew he saw her standing there. "Adam."

He held up a finger for her to wait. When he looked at her he couldn't suppress the knowing smile, or the I-told-you-so expression on his face. "Yes, Khara," he said, sounding very formal.

"Would you help me with the stove?" She tapped her foot on the floor and bit her lower lip. It hadn't been easy for her to ask him, and he probably wasn't going to make it any easier.

He narrowed his stare at her. "Gee, I can't seem to remember hearing the word 'please'."

"Please."

"Much better." He stood, came around his desk, and stopped in front of her, so close that their lips were inches apart. "This time it's going to cost you."

"Oh, yeah?" she said, hoping he couldn't tell how disturbing his nearness was.

"Yeah. It might cost you a loaf of bread." His gaze ran over her face. He walked over to the stove.

Khara again felt the mixture of annoyance and anticipation that his nearness caused. She suspected that was the effect he had wanted.

Within minutes Adam had the stove fixed and functioning. "A loose wire. That's all." As he pushed the stove back into place he said, "What did you ever do before you had me?"

Khara rolled her eyes. The man took too much credit. "I called the apartment manager."

"I'm sure he was eager to help you," Adam said. She remained silent as he walked by. Just past the counter, he paused and looked back at her. "Looks like you owe me for two things now. Rest assured, I'll collect." His lips curved slowly, but his eyes held something much different from humor.

Chapter Four

Adam hammered together two-by-fours for the framing of the shed. Sweat dripped profusely down the sides of his face. He wiped his forehead with the tails of his shirt and left a huge wet spot on the white material. It was too hot and sunny for this kind of work today.

Khara came out of the house carrying a tray of lemonade. "Thought you might be thirsty." She poured him a glass.

Adam had never tasted anything as good as that fresh-squeezed lemonade. He guzzled the glass. "Thanks," he said on an exhale.

"Are you making it the same size?" Khara asked.

"Bigger."

Her eyes widened in surprise, and a pleased smile crossed her lips. He watched her as she walked away over to her lounge chair. After she set the tray on the table next to her chair she removed her shorts and top, a two-piece bikini underneath.

Adam's mouth went dry. He couldn't

take his eyes off of her even if he'd wanted to. Forcing himself to look away, he picked up his hammer and took a nail from the pouch of his tool belt. He set the nail in place and raised the hammer. From the corner of his eye he saw Khara rubbing suntan lotion on her legs. He glanced over just as he pounded the hammer, striking his thumb.

"Ouch." He shook his hand, feeling his smashed thumbnail throb.

She moved her legs to the side of the chair and stood, then walked toward him like a goddess out for a stroll. "Would you mind rubbing sunscreen on my back?"

Adam licked his lips, took the bottle, and said, "Sure." She turned her back and lifted her dark red hair. It was thick and tousled in silky, heavy curls. Adam clenched his teeth and suppressed the urge to bury himself in it. He could almost feel his cheek rubbing against its thick softness.

His hand glided over her smooth skin, soft and alluring, warm to the touch. He was crazy, crazy to be letting her get to him this way.

Adam stared at her, the sunlight glistening golden highlights in her hair. He wondered if she knew how she could twist him up inside. Worst of it was — he let her.

He should walk away from her and her home, away from her beauty, away from her hardened glares. But he couldn't. He couldn't leave, just as he couldn't walk away at this moment.

"There," he said, his voice husky.

She turned back around and took the bottle from him. "Thank you."

As she strolled back to her chair and sat, Adam realized that she wasn't aware of her incredible beauty, which made her all the more beautiful. He doubted that she even cared she could catch a man's eye.

Adam went back to work, pounding nail after nail into the wood, hoping to rid himself of this extra energy, hoping he would be too tired to feel that constant ache in his heart every time he looked at her. His glance flew to her too many times, yet he couldn't stop himself.

Hours passed and Adam finished the framework and started on the trestles. A low hum of engines sounded down the drive. Adam checked his watch. 3:00. He looked at Khara, and a protectiveness swept over him. Before the men could park the rigs he rushed over, grabbed a towel lying on the ground, and covered her.

Behind the sunglasses her eyes opened, but didn't move. "What are you doing?"

"My men have returned," he said, thinking that explained everything.

"So?" She removed the towel and dropped it on the grass.

Adam grabbed it, shook it out, and laid it over her again.

She sat up, removed her glasses, and squinted at him. "Are you insane?"

"I was about to ask you the very same question." He jerked his head in the direction of the trucks and noticed the men climbing out of the cab. "Do you want the men to see you like" — he waved his hand up and down the length of her to indicate her body — "this?"

"Your men never come into the backyard. They won't come now."

"Guess again, because they are on their way." Adam stepped in front of her, blocking their view.

Ryan Avery reached Adam first and began to tell him how much they'd accomplished for the day. As he talked, Adam maneuvered Ryan toward the trucks. He couldn't help but notice the men glancing behind him at Khara. His teeth clenched. Suddenly, he was angry with her.

"Do you need help with the shed?" Ryan offered, moments after he'd glanced in Khara's direction.

"No. I can get it." Adam's hands fisted. "It'd be no trouble."

"I said I'd get it." Adam was glad when Ryan didn't push the matter any further. At his tone, none of the other men offered to help. After they drove away Adam returned to her. "They've all left."

She lowered the sunglasses on her nose and stared up at him. "Sometimes I'm convinced you're a raving lunatic."

Adam walked away. He didn't dare answer her because she was right. He had lost his mind when she'd entered his life. He hadn't acted the same, he hadn't had one good night's sleep, and had eaten better than a man had a right to. Yes, sir, he sure enough had lost his mind. He only hoped he would get it back soon, so he could think straight again.

Khara woke with a start. A thud struck the side of the house. The clock read midnight. The thump struck again almost as hard as her pounding heart. She held her breath. Someone was trying to break in. She pulled back the covers and slid her feet to the floor. As she stood, she wondered if her wobbly legs would hold her up.

An eerie feeling shivered down her spine.

She forced herself to take a breath. It came short and shallow. As she neared her bedroom door, which was open about a foot wide, a movement caught her gaze. There against the wall, she saw the silhouette creeping toward her room, the shadow large and ominous.

She was not alone!

Her entire body shook. Even her hair vibrated in fear. Of all the nights for Adam to go out with the men! He'd said he wouldn't be home until at least two in the morning.

Her hand shook as she reached for the baseball bat she kept behind her bedroom door. A picture frame scraped against the wall where it hung in the hallway only a few feet from her bedroom door, proving the shadow was more than her imagination. Moisture formed on the palms of her hand as she lifted the bat. She flattened her back against the wall next to her door. Summoning her courage, she peeked around the corner.

She sucked in a sharp breath. The person stood right in front of her, his back to her. She closed her eyes, certain the stranger could hear her breathing, could hear her heart hammering in her chest. Footsteps drifted away from her room and moved into the living room. She pushed the door wide. The hinges creaked in protest. Her heart nearly leaped out of her chest.

For what seemed like a lifetime, she waited and listened. A vase jostled on a coffee table in the living room. Mustering all her courage, she tiptoed barefoot out of her bedroom. Another step and she would have a full view of the living room. All she had to do was look. Her legs wobbled and nothing she could do would steady them.

Just as she was ready to take a step forward the shadow turned the corner, coming face-to-face with her. After the initial shock her instinct took over. She swung the bat, hoping to take advantage of the element of surprise, but she was too late. The shadow ducked.

Soon strong arms wrapped around her hands. She screamed and struggled to keep hold of her weapon, but her strength was no match for him. The bat was seized from her hands and clanked on the hardwood floor. Using her fists and feet, she thrust punches and kicks. In an instant, her arms were pinned at her side, her face pressed against a bare, muscular chest.

"Let go of me!"

"Would you calm down."

Khara froze. She knew that voice. Her muscles eased, then his arms loosened. She looked into Adam's face. In relief, she closed her eyes and leaned against him for support. The hairs on his chest tickled her cheek and she felt his stomach and chest muscles flex. An instant later, realizing what she was doing, she pulled out of his arms.

"What are you doing, sneaking in here like this? You're not supposed to cross the line. I thought you were a burglar. I —" A loud bang whammed against a window. She sucked in a sharp breath and met Adam's eyes. She didn't see a bit of fear in them, only concern.

He held his finger up for her to be quiet, then pointed to her bedroom. She was too scared to be left alone. She hurried to follow him and accidentally kicked him in the heel. When he suddenly halted, she collided into his back. He whirled around, his face inches from hers.

"I thought I told you to go in your room," he said in a strained whisper.

She couldn't — no, wouldn't — tell him how scared she was. "I thought . . . I could help."

He expelled a sigh. "Stay out of the way." Another thump in the family room

68

had Adam hurrying down the hallway. Khara followed. As soon as she reached the kitchen she flipped on the switch, lighting the family room. Adam lifted the blinds on the window. A blue tarp with a heavy rope attached to a limb of a tree, alongside the house, pounded against the glass.

Khara could hear the beat of her heart thudding in her ears and vibrating her body. "What is it?"

Adam looked at her. "The roofer didn't finish the job and covered the area with a tarp. Apparently he tied it off to a tree. The noises we heard were the branch, tarp, and rope beating against the roof and house."

"You told me that he would finish in one day."

"An emergency came up and he had to leave early."

Now that the danger had passed, her entire body shook and she had no way of controlling it. She had been scared, petrified, and all because Adam Mansfield hired a roofer. With her throat clogged with emotion, she forced her words out. "When are you going to be out of my house?"

Adam walked over to her until they

stood a foot apart and gazed into her face. She struggled to fight back the tears, the frustration. He pulled her into him, cradled her head against his chest, and held her tight. She closed her eyes and let the warmth of his embrace ease the tension from her stiff muscles. In her weak moment, she allowed a few tears of relief to escape.

He pulled back and cupped her face with his hands. With his thumbs he wiped away her tears. For a moment that seemed to last an eternity, he searched her eyes, then dropped his gaze to her lips. He hesitated as if he was resisting the temptation — then he bent his head.

He was going to kiss her. Khara's heart pounded like the beating of drums as she waited in anticipation. She wondered what his lips would feel like against hers and if they would be warm. Now when her pulse raced it was for an entirely different reason. Just as his lips touched hers the tarp, rope, and branch crashed through the window. Glass flew everywhere, startling them back to reality. Her eyes widened. For a moment they just looked in stunned silence at the shattered mess.

Khara struggled for a breath.

Adam's voice came out husky. "I guess

I'd better fix that."

Khara nodded, having a difficult time finding something to say. As he moved away from her, a cold chill settled on her skin. She rubbed her arms with her hands in a quick succinct motion. An irritation surfaced, causing her to frown. She'd allowed her attraction for him to show. Suddenly Khara felt very vulnerable.

"I'm sorry about all of this," Adam said as he untied the rope from the branch and tarp. "I didn't mean for you to get frightened."

"I wasn't frightened." Khara answered quickly, too quickly.

"Yeah, well, whatever," Adam muttered over his shoulder. His tone indicated he didn't believe her.

"What do you expect?" Khara said defensively. "You told me you wouldn't be home until the early morning hours." A surge of jealousy rushed through her veins at the thought of Adam out with another woman. A hesitant pause filled the room before she asked, "Why did you come home so early?"

For a brief second his hands froze, then he continued untying knots in the rope. He glanced at her before he absorbed his attention back to the rope again. "I don't know. I guess I was bored."

A pause lingered. "I'll help you clean this mess up."

"That's okay." His response came out swiftly. "I'll get it. Go to bed."

She nodded and turned to return to her room. When she reached the kitchen he said, "I'll patch this tonight and replace the window tomorrow."

"Okay." As she looked back at him, she caught him casting a glance over at her and the corners of his mouth turning upward. A tingling sensation danced along her skin — no matter how hard she tried to suppress it.

Adam let the cool wind blow through the window onto his bare skin as he removed the large pieces of glass. He needed something to cool him off. Holding Khara in his arms felt good, too good. Every time he was around her a swell of protectiveness and tenderness all rolled into one emerged inside him, a new and different emotion. He felt so comfortable around her, and had since the moment they'd met. Sure, it could be because he'd heard about her for years and seen her pictures, but it was more than that.

Each time his glance dropped to her lips

he felt a powerful urge to kiss her. Moments ago he'd come close to doing just that. Now he knew — anything less would never do.

What was happening to him? He hadn't thought of a woman in this way in a long time, if ever. All his life he'd made certain that a woman never controlled him. He loved his mother dearly, but he would never allow any woman to boss him around the way his mother had his father. She'd always gotten her way. There was never compromise between them. His father had always been wrong and she'd been right. Adam forced out a breath. In the past, the minute a woman had started to put demands on him, he'd been out the door. With Khara, it was different. He found he wanted to please her, to give to her. Maybe because she gave so freely in return. Yet, everything he did seemed to irritate her.

He might have grown up on the land, but patience was never one of his virtues. When he saw something or someone he wanted, he went after them. With Khara he found himself holding back because he knew that if he went after her, there would be no turning back.

Adam wanted to do something about his

growing feelings for her, but what?

He'd gone to the tavern with the guys to seek out other women and ended up leaving early. Sure he'd had offers, but those women failed so miserably in comparison to Khara. They lacked the depth and quality she had. After he'd left the tavern Adam knew that no substitute would ever do. None of the women in Morton, Washington could satisfy the craving that hounded him. No one but this auburn-haired, green-eyed beauty.

No matter what he did, nothing eased the agony of wanting to be with her and knowing he'd have to let go of his fears in order to have her. He'd done that once before with a woman and she'd left him. Of course, looking back on it, he couldn't blame Pamela for leaving. She had wanted a different life, a life in the city with lots of people and lots of things to do. That wasn't the life for him. Adam had grown up a logger's son, hunting in the mountains, and living in a small town. He liked a slow-paced way of life, where he knew almost everyone in town and they knew him. He'd had a taste of that "other" life when he'd gone to college near Seattle, but all four years he'd longed to return home to the sanctity of the woods.

Adam retrieved the vacuum and cleaned up the bits of glass that were scattered on the floor, window ledge, and chair. A picture of Khara appeared in his mind, looking scared and vulnerable in her nightgown. A chuckle bubbled from his throat. She'd nearly taken his head off with that bat. The instant he'd wrestled the weapon from her, he'd felt her pulse bound in her wrist, just as it had the other times he'd touched her.

When she'd struggled in his arms and he'd been able to restrain her, she had stirred something in him. He'd had to dig deep not to turn her within his arms and kiss her.

He felt himself sinking much deeper and quicker than he'd expected, or wanted.

When he stapled the plastic into place the cool air subsided, but the ache inside burned just as hot as before. He wished he could find something, *anything,* to stamp out the attraction he felt for Khara. It scared him to death!

Maybe he'd been wrong insisting on living here. Maybe he'd put her in danger. Someone for the past several months had been sabotaging his large machinery. He couldn't think of anyone who would deliberately try to hurt him and his business, but someone was. From Khara's family room, he could see directly into the fenced area where the equipment was parked. He intended to nab the person. Then there would be consequences to pay.

Adam turned out the lights before he climbed back into bed. For a while he lay there, his hands resting behind his head, and stared up at the ceiling. The wind gusted outside, flapping the plastic that covered the window. In a sudden burst, rain thundered down on the house. A drop plopped on Adam's forehead, followed by several more.

A new leak.

A groan slipped through his lips. Another sleepless night. He wished he could be with Khara and hold her close, smell the sweet scent of her perfume, and feel the soft texture of her hair.

He'd thought that moving in with her had been the answer to his problems, but it was giving him more to deal with than he wanted.

After two weeks of job searching all Khara wanted to do was spend Friday night alone with a good book, a cup of tea, and a chocolate bar. It had been another week of job rejections, with a glimmer of hope coming when Aunt Bea called and notified her that one of the teachers at the early intervention preschool in town had given notice that she would not be returning next school year. Khara had filled out an application and whizzed it along with her résumé over to the administration office faster than she could blink her eyes. She needed this job, desperately. And according to Bea, the school didn't have anyone in mind, which gave her a fair chance at getting it.

Khara slipped her shoes off, curled her feet underneath her, and opened the book. She didn't read more than a page when the kitchen door opened and a group of men entered, talking, one of them she recognized as Adam. Seconds later he walked down the hall, peeked in her bedroom, then found her in the living room.

"There you are," he said.

"You sure make a habit of trespassing." When he frowned she added, "Crossing the taped line."

His mouth relaxed into a smile. "Oh, that. You weren't serious about that, were you?"

"Yes."

Adam glanced away and shifted from one foot to the other in his stance. He looked back at her, a pleading expression on his face. "Would you make us a few sandwiches?"

"Are you having a late business meeting?"

"Something like that."

She nodded. "Sure." Khara set her book down and went into the kitchen, noticing the men had seated themselves around a table they'd set up in the middle of the family room. Including Adam, there were five men. She hoped this meeting would be over soon. She longed to have her solitude back, her quiet, boring evenings that she normally used for studying or preparing for the next day's class.

She finished with the sandwiches, poured a bag of potato chips in a bowl, placed freshly baked cookies on a plate, and set everything on the table. The second she saw a deck of cards, poker chips, cigars, and beer, she knew this wasn't any business meeting. An irritation immediately ignited in the pit of her stomach.

"Khara, this is John Hinkle, Matt Campbell, Ben Johnson, and Brian Elliot. Guys, this is Khara Thompson, my roommate."

Khara cringed at the word "roommate." Like she had a choice in Adam moving in?

"We're the L.B.C.s," John said, his blue eyes sparkling in a flirtatious manner, his lips curving in a smile, matching the handsome, model-like features of his face. John didn't have the ruggedness to his looks that Adam did but he definitely was attractive, even wearing a worn baseball shirt and jeans.

"What does L.B.C. stand for?"

John looked pleased she asked. "The Last Bachelors' Club."

"Well, if you'll excuse me, I think I'll go join my bachelorette club."

"Why don't you join us?" John offered, gaining glares from a couple of the men, including Adam.

"Yeah, why don't you?" Brian chimed in.

"No, thank you." She smiled to be polite, then looked at Adam. "May I have a word with you?" Not giving him a chance to refuse, she walked away.

"You're in trouble now, Adam," Ben said, followed by a belly laugh.

"I think Adam's dead meat," Matt added.

Even after she reached the living room the men continued to make comments followed by laughter. She folded her arms over her chest and drummed her fingers. "You told me that you were having a business meeting."

His brows came together. "We talk about business."

"While you play cards and drink beer."

"We don't do anything wrong," he said a little defensively.

She took a deep breath in an effort to control her temper. It didn't work. She paced the floor in front of him. "First you force me to let you move in here. Then you move in before me, try to steal my bedroom, and put all your furniture in my house. If that's not enough, your dump trucks have arrived here at five every morning, your men rev the engines, then they run in and out of my house, and on top of that you hire a roofer, without my permission, and he disrupts my lesson." She stopped in front of him and faced him, her eyes blazing, and lowered her voice to a strained whisper. "Now you have the absolute nerve to have a poker party in my house."

"We'll be quiet. I promise."

"Why can't you play poker at one of their houses?"

"Because tonight's my turn and you have a huge family room. None of the other guys have a place this big."

Khara couldn't believe his lame excuse. She felt on the verge of exploding. "You are not playing poker here again. Do we understand each other?"

Adam dipped his head and when he met her eyes he said, "I'm sorry. I should have asked." He took a step to leave, paused, and looked back at her. "Thanks for making the sandwiches."

After Adam left, Khara continued to stare at the opening into the kitchen. She couldn't see the men from where she stood, but she sure could hear them loud and clear.

"So what's the deal between you and Khara?" John asked. "Are you two sharing more than a house?"

"Yeah, come clean," another man said.

"It's nothing like that, you guys. She's not that kind of woman. She's a schoolteacher."

Clear from the living room Khara could hear the defensiveness in Adam's tone.

"She's the prettiest schoolteacher I've ever seen," John said. A couple of the other men grunted an agreement.

Khara smiled to herself. She'd been told she was pretty before, but usually from her five- and six-year-olds, not from grown men. Her father had always told her that she had a natural beauty that required very little makeup so she never tried to fix herself up unless she had to. She preferred a casual and comfortable look.

"She's one good cook," Adam said, a ring of pride in his voice. "I think I've gained ten pounds since I moved in."

"Let me get this straight," Brian said. "You have a gorgeous woman living under the same roof as you, she's sweet, and is an excellent cook, and you haven't even asked her out?"

Khara waited in anticipation to hear Adam's answer, which seemed to take forever.

"Come on, you guys. She's my mother's best friend's niece."

"So?" Brian persisted.

"Are we here to play poker or talk?" Adam said, his tone harsh and defensive.

"So you won't mind if I ask her out?" John said.

A pause lingered before Adam replied, "Why would I mind? I told you there was nothing between us."

Disappointment pinched at Khara's heart. Apparently, she'd been reading his signs all wrong. In fact there had been no signs. Adam didn't have any feelings for her. She felt like a fool thinking he might. She had been right, guarding her feelings. Trying to ignore the knot forming in her stomach, she returned to the couch and read. She blocked out any further conversation the men had. She'd heard enough.

After an hour passed John came into the living room. "Good book?"

Khara looked up. "There's a bathroom in the family room."

John flashed her one of his brilliant smiles, his teeth perfectly straight and white. "I found what I was looking for." He gazed at her.

"Do you need more sandwiches?"

He hesitated and his smile wavered before he said, "I was wondering if you'd like to go out with me to a movie or dinner — or both — sometime?"

Khara's heart started to thud. She hadn't anticipated this. How long had it been since a man had asked her out? And how long had it been since she'd accepted? Her mouth felt dry. She had to start dating again. She had to try, even if it meant opening herself up to rejection. Otherwise she'd live a life of a monk, lonely and alone.

Dragging in a breath she said, "I'd love to."

John's wide grin returned and his eyes danced with confidence. "I'll call you."

"Okay." Khara forced herself to smile

despite the nerves rushing to every limb in her body.

Adam joined them, his gaze flying between Khara and John. "Are you going to play cards or not?"

"Sure," John said and walked away.

Adam stood there for a minute and stared at Khara. She ignored him and pretended to read her book, yet the words blurred on the page. A tingling surfaced in her stomach. Inwardly she reprimanded herself for allowing him to so easily stir her emotions.

"Are you going out with him?"

Khara stared at the book. "Uh-huh."

"When?"

She shrugged and glanced at him. With his arms folded over his broad chest he looked anything but happy. He opened his mouth as if ready to say something, then clamped his lips together and left.

Khara wasn't stupid enough to believe Adam was actually showing signs of jealousy, especially after he so freely told John and the other men he wasn't interested in her. Focusing back on her book, she read her romance and wondered if fairy tales really did come true.

Chapter Five

As Khara drove her car into the garage it coughed and sputtered until she turned the motor off. She got out and carried a bag of groceries into the house.

Without looking up from his desk, Adam said, "You want me to take a look at your car?"

"Why?"

"Why?" he said as if she were crazy. "I could hear you coming clear down the street."

"If there's anything wrong with my car I'll fix it." She didn't give him a chance to respond as she stepped back into the garage to retrieve more groceries.

Seconds later Adam joined her. As he hefted two bags in his arms he said, "I really wouldn't mind."

Khara halted and pivoted to look at him. "I said I'd fix it. Besides, how hard can it be if a man can fix it." She smiled sweetly.

Adam put on an easy smile, unfazed by her comment. He said nothing as they finished unloading the bags. He returned to his office area and let Khara put the groceries away. Before she'd finished he returned and set a book on the counter. "You might need this."

Khara glanced at the book that had "Chilton" written across the top of it. "What is it?"

"A book on the mechanics of your car." He flipped through the pages for her to see. "It even has pictures and diagrams for you to follow."

She noticed the car pictured on the book was the same make and model as hers. "Where'd you get this book?"

"A friend of mine owns an auto parts store."

That really didn't explain how he got the book, but Khara didn't intend to pursue the matter. After she finished folding the paper bags and putting them away she picked up the book, went out to the garage, opened the hood of her car, and started to read. She nearly fell asleep after finishing the first page.

She glanced at the garage door to the house and contemplated whether she should ask Adam for help or not. She decided against it. The last thing she needed was for Adam to tell her she owed him — again!

Khara remained in the garage for the next hour and skimmed through the book. She recognized a few of the parts of the engine, like the air filter and where to put the oil. She mastered how to pull the oil stick out, wipe it clean, put it back in the oil hole, and back out again to measure the level of oil. Unfortunately, that was about all she understood. She not only had no talent in auto mechanics, she had no interest.

She slipped back into the house and hoped Adam wouldn't hear her. As she took a step, heading out of the kitchen, Adam asked, "Did you figure it out?"

She whirled around and folded her arms over her chest. "What I figured out is that I'm going to take it to a mechanic in town."

"Why would you hire a mechanic when I've offered to work on it for free?" Adam drew his brows together, clearly not pleased. He got out of his chair and stepped into the kitchen as if he wanted to hear a good explanation.

Khara decided to tell him the truth. "Nothing is ever free with you. If you're not asking for more than I can give with your little innuendos, then you want food. You're eating me out of house and home."

A grin curved the corners of his mouth. "What's wrong with a good appetite?"

"Nothing. I don't know how you can eat so much and not have an ounce of fat on you."

His grin turned into a full-fledged smile. "You noticed whether I have fat on me or not, huh?"

Heat rushed to Khara's face. Without even trying she'd disclosed much more to him than she had intended to. She dropped her gaze to the ground, wishing the color in her face wouldn't brighten like a floodlight.

"What else have you noticed about me?"

Khara wondered if his head would swell to the size of his ego. "What else is there to notice?"

He placed his hand over his heart in an exaggerated manner as if she'd wounded him. "There's my great smile, intelligent mind, and charming personality."

She rolled her eyes. "Sorry, I missed those."

He stepped over to her, his gaze meeting hers. "I haven't missed your good qualities." He lifted a curl of her hair, twisted it on his finger, and said, "Like how your hair glistens in the sun, how your eyes turn a darker shade of green when you're angry, and . . ." He loosened his finger from her hair and ran it along her cheek. ". . . how your skin turns a delicate shade of pink when you are upset or embarrassed."

Khara searched his eyes. Was he serious, or toying with her? She couldn't tell. She turned her head and his hand dropped to his side. Instinctively she was on guard. Adam was a tease, but she wouldn't buy into his flattery. He'd told John to ask her out on a date. "I'll find my own mechanic in town, thank you," she said in a formal, distant manner.

For a flicker of a second he drew his brows together as if confused. All signs of a smile fled from his face. He pressed his lips together and gave a sharp nod. "If that's what you want."

Even after he turned and left Khara could still feel the wall of tension between them. Maybe it was better this way. It would make it easier for her to guard her feelings and not get so easily swept into his charm. She would stay away from Adam Mansfield.

Far away from him!

When Khara's alarm went off Tuesday morning she jumped out of bed. She had an interview this morning and she didn't want anything to go wrong. After she showered, she carefully applied her makeup, tied her hair back in a ponytail, and dressed in her pastel green suit. She slipped on her high-heel shoes and earrings, then checked her watch.

The night before she had put all the papers in her briefcase that the interview panel might want to discuss, covering techniques she'd used with dyslexic children and one that she'd developed. She knew she did good work, but that never guaranteed getting a job. Nerves danced in her stomach. Normally she wouldn't be this anxious, but she *needed* this job. She also wanted this job, more than she cared to admit. She loved working with children. It was her life. Without it she didn't know what she would do. She could always work in a regular classroom, substituting, since she'd been certified, but her real passion was helping the children who came into this life with a disadvantage.

She laughed. She could relate to these children better now, since Adam Mansfield always seemed to put her at a disadvantage. At least today he couldn't make her life more difficult. She would go to her interview and just for a few hours forget he had intruded into her comfortable world.

Khara headed into the garage and tossed her purse and briefcase in the front seat on the passenger side, then opened the garage door. For a moment she stared, furious, at the four vehicles that blocked her from getting out. *Not today. Please, not today.* She suppressed the hysteria boiling just below the surface and sought out Adam.

He wasn't at his desk, in the house, or working on the machinery. What would she do if he wasn't here? She checked her watch. She had twenty minutes to get there. The drive into town would take most of that up. Panic swirled inside her, knotting her stomach. She stepped out the back door, her hands shaking.

A movement caught her eye as she spotted Adam painting the side of the shed. "I've been looking for you everywhere."

He gave her that easy grin of his and raised his brows. "You missed me, huh?"

Khara ignored his humor. "Your employees have parked behind my car. I need you to move them right away."

He scanned the length of her. "Why are you dressed up?"

"I have an interview for a teaching job this morning." The stress she felt came through in her tone and in the stiffened muscles in her body.

Adam's smile faded into a frown. "I can't move their cars. I don't have their keys."

Khara tried to say the word "what" but only a gust of air came out. She checked her watch. "I have to be at this interview in fifteen minutes. Give me the keys to your truck. I'll drive that."

"My men took my truck to the logging site."

Khara couldn't suppress the hysteria she felt any longer. Tears of frustration surfaced in her eyes; her voice rose in volume. "What am I supposed to do? I need this job. Do you know how hard it is to find a teaching job right now?"

Calmly, Adam raised his hands, palms outward. "I'll get you there."

"How?"

"In one of my company vehicles."

She frowned. "I didn't know you had a company vehicle." Without giving him a chance to reply she nodded and said, "Okay. I'll get my purse and briefcase, and meet you out front." Khara ran in the house as fast as she could in her high heels, grabbed her things out of her car, and rushed out the front door.

She abruptly halted.

Adam sat behind the wheel of a huge hauling truck, carrying a dozer on the back! He hopped down from the cab that looked to be ten stories high and came around.

Khara glanced at the door of the cab, several feet off the ground, then at her high heels. "You've got to be joking. Don't you have anything else?"

"Nope."

A sigh of disgust burst from her mouth. "How am I supposed to get up there?"

"I'm going to help you." Adam led the way to the truck, hopped up the two steps, opened the door, then jumped to the ground. "Come on." He motioned with a wave of his hand.

Khara hiked her knee-length skirt up her thighs, then stretched her foot to the first step. Adam held one of her hands, and she gripped the door tightly with the other. She felt like she was doing the splits. On the step, she wavered and lost her balance. Suddenly she felt two hands around her waist, bracing her. She snapped at him. "Do you mind?"

"Would you rather fall?" Adam pushed and grunted as if she weighed three hundred pounds.

Khara fell forward into the cab of the

truck, her body lying across the seat, her legs sticking out and her feet kicking in the air. She dumped her briefcase on the truck floor, and grabbed for anything to hang on to to pull herself into a sitting position.

Adam beat her to it, opening the driver's side, sliding inside, and grasping her hand, hauling her into the cab. A ripple of laughter burst from him.

Khara struggled to sit up, then tugged on her skirt and jacket. "I don't see what's so funny."

"If you saw yourself from my view you would."

The roar of the engine drowned out any further conversation, and Adam shifted the vehicle into gear and drove like a madman into town. They stopped at a red light as they neared the school.

"Why don't I get out here?" Khara said. "I'll walk the rest of the way." The last thing she wanted was to arrive at her interview in a huge truck, hauling a dozer. What an impression that would make!

"Nonsense. It's only two blocks away. I don't want you to walk all that way in your high heels. Besides, you're late as it is." The light changed to green. Shifting the truck into a lower gear, Adam drove to the school and pulled up to the front.

Khara hoped and prayed no one on the panel would see her. She opened the door and stared at the ground far below her feet. If she jumped she'd break her heels for sure.

A second later Adam stood at her door, his arms outstretched to lift her out. Before she could protest, he hauled her out and planted her on the ground. Again, she pulled on her jacket and skirt and straightened the strap of her purse over her shoulder. Adam climbed up, retrieved her briefcase, then handed it to her.

"I'm going to go to the café for a cup of coffee. How long do you think you'll be?" he said.

"An hour."

He nodded. "Good luck."

Khara tried to smile but one never formed. She was a nervous wreck. Taking a deep breath, she tried to calm herself down. As she took a step to leave, Adam said, "You look really nice." This time she managed an appreciative smile, then hurried into the building.

When Khara arrived at the office the applicant before her was still being interviewed, which gave Khara time to gather her thoughts. Twenty minutes later they called her into the room. There were three people on the panel, a man and two women, all of them with notepads and pens in front of them.

"I'm Kevin Sutton, the school administrator. This is Angela Ingall, she's head of our preschool program, and this is Beth Parson, who teaches in the early intervention program with the three- and four-year-old group. We are looking for someone to teach the five- and six-year-olds and integrate them into a normal school curriculum."

Khara shook their hands, hoping she'd wiped at least most of the perspiration off her palms. Kevin gestured for her to sit at the table opposite them and gave her time to get her paperwork out of her briefcase. She glanced at the glass of water sitting on the table in front of her. She would have loved to take a drink, but her hand would shake too much. With her luck she would probably slosh it all over the table and papers. Instead she swallowed, her mouth dry.

"Why don't you start by telling us about your background?" Kevin said.

Once Khara got started talking about her work she began to relax. She was nearly through with her interview when she noticed a reflection of a red light

96

flashing off the walls in the room. The panel saw it too, and Kevin interrupted the interview to look out the window.

"It seems there's a truck blocking the driveway where the school's training their new bus drivers. The police must be here to get the truck moved or towed away. I'd better go check on it. I'll be right back."

Khara joined the other two women at the window, then closed her eyes. Sure enough, Adam was disrupting her life again. She searched the area and saw him crossing the street, strolling toward his truck. He spoke a few minutes with the police officer and both of them laughed. Then Kevin joined them.

Please, Adam, don't tell Kevin Sutton you're waiting for me. No sooner did she think it than Adam pointed toward the building. Khara groaned inwardly. Why did this man make it his calling to disrupt her life? When she saw Kevin enter the building she returned to her seat and waited.

As soon as Kevin pushed through the door he said, "I guess we'd better call this interview short so we can get that truck moved." He shook Khara's hand. "Thanks for coming. We'll let you know who we select in a few days."

Dread and disappointment washed over Khara. She didn't have a prayer of getting this job. She just knew it. Despite the lump that had formed in her throat she smiled, thanked them, and left.

The second she saw Adam, anger consumed her. He opened the door for her. She threw her briefcase in, followed by her purse, and with very little effort by Adam, she climbed in the cab. She was so furious she could probably climb Mt. Everest right now, high heels and all.

After Adam sat behind the steering wheel a heavy silence filled the cab. He glanced at her. "Everything okay?"

She shot him a cool look, but said nothing.

They didn't exchange a single word the entire drive home. The second he stopped the vehicle she opened the door. With purse and briefcase in hand, she jumped to the ground. Pain shot up her ankle. Hobbling to the house, she went into her bedroom and slammed the door.

Khara changed into jeans, T-shirt, and sneakers. There was only one way to calm herself down. When she went into the kitchen she noticed Adam sitting at his desk. She could feel him staring at her, but she refused to look over at him.

After several minutes of silence he said, "When's lunch going to be ready?"

His comment fueled her anger. She responded by slamming a pot on the stove.

Adam charged into the kitchen and braced his hands on the lunch counter. "Are you going to tell me what you're so upset about?"

She glared at him straight in the eyes. "You deliberately ruined my interview."

"What are you talking about?"

"That little scene you pulled."

He frowned. "You mean my truck being in the way?"

"Of course I mean that. My interview was cut short because of you and that stupid truck."

The wrinkles around his eyes softened as a look of surprise crossed his face. "I'm sorry. I told Kevin I'd move it as soon as you were done."

"You were blocking the way for the buses."

Adam folded his arms over his muscular chest. "It's not easy to find a parking spot for a fully loaded hauling truck."

It irritated Khara that he had a valid point, but she didn't intend to let him off easy. "I don't have a prayer of getting this job and it's all because of you. If your employees hadn't parked in my driveway none of this would have happened."

"Look, I'll make it up to you."

"No! You won't do anything else but stay out of my life." She saw hurt flash in his brown eyes as soon as the words flew out of her mouth. Guilt niggled at her.

Adam said nothing as he pivoted around and returned to his desk. Thirty minutes later she set his lunch on the counter and left. She didn't want to say anything else that might wound his feelings, and she was mad enough to do that very thing.

Adam shuffled through stacks of paper. He had a lot of work to catch up on. He'd stayed out of the house, and Khara's way, for several days, hoping she'd calm down. He glanced up as John walked into the family room. "What are you all dressed up for?" Adam asked.

"I'm taking Khara out to dinner."

A ripple of jealousy shot through Adam's gut. He tried to smile, but only a faint one formed. "Where you taking her?"

"Rainbow Falls Terrace."

"That's pretty fancy." His hands flexed as he rested them on the desk.

John shrugged. "You can't take a classy woman like Khara to McDonald's."

Adam didn't agree. He thought Khara would fit right in whether it be at a burger joint or a nice restaurant. That's what he liked about her. She could fit in at any place with any crowd, even with *his* friends. "Are you going somewhere afterward?"

"That depends."

"On?" Adam knew what John was going to say and the knot formed tighter in his belly.

"Khara."

Adam stood, his hands formed in tight balls at his sides. "Khara's not like that. She'll come right home." He didn't want to sound defensive or protective, but he did, and there was nothing that could stop him from feeling that way.

John narrowed his stare at Adam. "I thought you said there was nothing going on between you two."

"There isn't." Darn, he answered way too quickly.

For a moment, John stared at Adam, confusion written all over his face. Adam met John's eyes, his stare never wavering.

"I'm ready," Khara said, stepping into the room and breaking the tension.

Adam ran a glance over her. She wore a cream-colored dress, her hair hanging long, just the way he liked it, and she'd applied a small amount of makeup that accentuated her long lashes, the curve of her lips, the angles of her cheekbones, and the vibrant green of her eyes. She was beautiful. Breathtaking. Before he could stop himself he said, "You look wonderful."

Khara smiled at the compliment.

"Yeah, you do," John said, then glanced at his watch. "We should be going. Our reservations are in a half-hour." He guided Khara to the door.

Adam followed, unable to take his eyes off of John's hand on the small of Khara's back. He resisted the urge to rip John's arm away. Instead, he curled his fingers deeper inside his palms and squeezed.

"Your dinner's in the oven," Khara said over her shoulder.

After the door shut, Adam stepped into the living room and watched John open the door to his black sedan for Khara. He didn't miss how John took an extra-long look at her as she sat down. John must have wanted to impress Khara, taking her to a fancy restaurant and opening the door for her. These were courtesies he hadn't seen John do very often for a woman.

Adam suddenly felt like lashing out at something, anything. Each evening he looked forward to discussing his day with

Khara over dinner. She listened, really listened, and cared. He'd never had a woman do that before, not even his mother. And he enjoyed hearing about the progress she was making with Taylor. The children she worked with had difficult challenges in their lives, but he knew that Khara would somehow make it easier for them.

The other night when Khara had told him she'd wanted him out of his life, the words had stung. He couldn't remember hurting like that before. Not even with Pamela. He hadn't quite figured out how to prevent it from happening again. Yet no matter how Khara had hurt him, nothing seemed to stop him from wanting to spend time with her, talk with her, and be around her. He had to fight this attraction. She'd be better off with John. Adam released a long, slow sigh. That wasn't true. John wasn't the marrying type, and Adam wanted to protect Khara from a potential heartache.

Adam had vowed to never allow himself to become emotionally involved with a woman again and that's exactly what he was doing with Khara. His feelings for her grew by the day and it seemed as if he had no control over them. She was different from women he'd dated. She made him laugh. He liked her directness and honesty. Most of all, he liked the fact that the mere sight of her made his head spin, in a way no other woman ever had.

He thrust his hands into his pockets, threw his head slightly back, and continued to stare out the window. Why didn't he feel the rough texture of the rope circling his neck and tightening? Normally he did when he started developing feelings for a woman. So why wasn't it happening this time with Khara? He wanted it to happen. He wanted to feel trapped, to feel that his freedom was being snatched from him. That way, it made it so much easier to flee without looking back.

He returned to the family room, sat down at his desk, and stared at the papers in front of him that waited for his signature. The bid deadline was tomorrow. The last thing he felt like doing was filling it out. He pushed away from the desk and wandered into the kitchen. Opening the oven, he pulled out the plate and set it on the counter, grabbed a soda from the refrigerator, and sat down.

The quiet in the house nearly screamed out at him. A loneliness settled over him. Before Khara had come into his life, he'd spent many nights alone, and he'd never minded it then, so why now? Darn, he didn't want to feel this way. But he did. He ached to have her here, to fill that emptiness inside, an emptiness that had been with him for years, yet he had denied existed — an emptiness he'd so suddenly become aware of.

It was hard enough to realize that he didn't want Khara the same way he had wanted other women, but to realize how vulnerable he was becoming and in such a short time!

Throughout the evening Adam glanced out the front window, checked his watch, and listened for the sound of a motor outside. Even the baseball game on television couldn't distract him from his thoughts. As the hours grew late he heard the humming of an engine and went into the living room to investigate. He peeked out the front window and watched Khara and John walk up to the front porch. Hurrying, Adam whipped open the door. He held no apology in his voice when he said, "I thought I heard someone out here."

He remained standing there, his arms folded over his chest, his feet the width of his shoulders. "Have a nice dinner? The one Khara made for me tonight sure was good."

"She mentioned she likes to cook," John said, "and offered to make me dinner on our next date."

Adam was irritated that she had agreed to see John again, and cook for him. He wanted her to save that talent for him. Gripping Khara's arm he said, "It's late, Khara, and Taylor's coming over an hour earlier tomorrow. You should get to bed."

John grasped her other arm. "Adam, we're not finished." He rolled his eyes and jerked his head, hinting for Adam to leave.

Adam's stare met John's and never faltered as he drew Khara back to him. "Khara's tired. She needs her rest."

Anger reddened John's face and his nostrils flared. Using more force, he yanked her back and she collided into him.

"You've been out all night," Adam said, and pulled her back to him.

"Khara can make her own decisions." John tugged again.

The two men glared at each other.

"Stop it. I feel like a wishbone." Khara jerked her arms free from both men. Looking at Adam she said, "Would you excuse us?"

Reluctantly, Adam took one step back, and waited.

Khara gave him a warning glare before

she snapped the door shut. Seconds later she opened it and entered. After it shut she leaned her back against the door, her arms folded over her chest, and glared. "Have you lost your mind?"

"John's not the right man for you." The words just blurted out of his mouth. He looked away.

"If I want your opinion I'll ask for it." She waited until he looked at her, then narrowed her stare at him. "Did my aunt put you up to this?"

Adam curled his fingers in his hands to keep from touching her, to keep from pulling her into his arms and kissing her, to keep from telling her that he missed her. Instead of answering her question he said, "Did he kiss you good night?"

"Yes. Are you going to send Bea a report on my evening?"

He didn't answer.

"Well, you can tell her that we had a lovely dinner, took a stroll along the falls and talked, stopped for ice cream, and came home. John was a complete gentleman the entire time." She pushed away from the door and stepped by him. "Unlike some people I know."

That was a first for John, to act like a gentleman even on the first date. The tension in Adam's shoulders eased. Before she could enter her bedroom he said, "I made coffee. Would you like a cup?"

She turned and a smile lifted the corners of her mouth. "I thought you said I should get to bed."

Adam watched her pivot, enter her bedroom, and shut the door. Disappointed, he decided to go to bed. Could his reaction be nothing more than brotherly concern for her? Yeah, that had to be it. It just had to be!

Chapter Six

As Khara worked with Taylor at the counter she kept glancing at Adam's empty desk. He'd gone out to look over a road that needed to be replaced. A warm, tingling feeling rose in her chest as she thought about the concern Adam had shown for her the previous night. The last time anyone had waited up for her was when she had lived at home with her parents, years ago.

She wondered if Aunt Bea had asked Adam to look out for her, or if he'd done it on his own. He never would answer that question. Was he protecting Aunt Bea or himself? Last night she'd fallen asleep with a smile on her face, thinking about how Adam opened the front door before John could kiss her.

Taylor tugged on her sleeve and pointed to his paper. "Good. Very good." She signed the words with her hands and spoke at the same time. As the lesson continued the phone rang.

"Khara, it's Aunt Bea. I was wondering if you could help us out."

"Sure. What do you need?"

"Our Ladies Auxiliary is having a fundraiser for the Grange. We're asking available ladies to make a picnic lunch basket and sell it to the highest bidder. Then you get to eat lunch with the young man who buys your basket."

"Oh, Aunt Bea," Khara said on a groan. "It sounds like *I'm* the one that will be on the auction block, not my basket."

"No, no, dear. The baskets will all be numbered. The man who buys your basket won't know who made it until they pay for it. That way it's more of a pleasant surprise."

When Khara didn't say anything Bea added, "It would really help us out. The money will go toward the children's activities at the Grange."

All Bea had to say was the word "children," and Khara was hooked. She suspected Bea knew that too. "Sure. I'd love to."

"Wonderful. I knew I could count on you. Be sure to put a big pink bow on the basket handle for decoration." The line grew quiet, then Bea said, "Is Adam there? Dolores wants to talk to him."

"No, he's out and I don't know when he'll be back."

"Okay, dear. She can talk to him later." Bea gave Khara the details of when, where, and what time, then hung up.

Khara placed the receiver in its cradle and sat there for a moment wondering if this wasn't another attempt by her aunt to set her up on a blind date. The request sounded legitimate enough. She gave her head a slight shake. She was becoming much too suspicious. Glancing over at Taylor, she went back to work, realizing that she felt more comfortable around five-year-olds than she did thirty-three-year-olds.

"Did you hear that John Hinkle took Khara out the other night?" Bea said.

"No, I didn't." Dolores frowned in deep thought and tapped a finger on her cheek. "You know, we could use that to our advantage."

"What do you mean?"

"John and Adam are best friends, but they also tend to compete against each other."

"So?" Bea didn't like the mischievous smile that formed on Dolores's lips.

"So we'll invite John to the auction and have him bid on Khara's basket. Adam will want to outdo John and bid against him.

Then Adam and Khara will have lunch to-gether."

"What if Adam doesn't bid on Khara's basket? Maybe we should give up this crazy idea of playing matchmaker."

Dolores folded her arms over her chest. "No. I won't. I know what's best for my son. Marrying Khara is best." She motioned for Bea to follow her out the door.

"Where are we going?"

"To accidentally run into John and let him know which basket is Khara's," Dolores said.

Darn, he was late.

Adam checked his watch for the third time. The Grange auction had started twenty minutes ago. Not only had he promised his mother he'd be there, but he wanted to bid on Khara's basket before another man did. Just the thought twisted his stomach into a knot. He pulled into the gravel parking lot, jumped out, and hurried inside.

Many people filled the Grange, and a table near the podium, full of baskets, had yet to be auctioned off. Adam searched for Khara's, but there were too many to distin-guish hers from the others. He stood in the back by the wall and scanned the crowd.

His mother and Bea stood near the podium, handing out the baskets and collecting the money, while an old friend of the family, Sam Tucker, acted as the auctioneer.

In the crowd the deep rich red of Khara's hair caught his eye. Adam strained to see who she was talking to, then he instantly recognized John. As Adam made his way through the throng of people adrenaline pumped through his veins, the same feeling he got each time he competed in sports or business. As he reached them he stood on the opposite side of Khara.

"I'm surprised to see you here, John," Adam said, then glanced at Khara and couldn't help but grin when she flashed him one of her smiles.

"Where've you been?" John said.

"We had another 'problem' with our grader."

John nodded in understanding. "You still going to be able to bid on the junction road?"

"I hope so." Adam turned to Khara. "Has your basket gone up for auction yet?"

"No."

"Which one is it?"

Her seductive lips curved upward. Adam had to force himself to briefly look away.

"I'm not supposed to tell. Aunt Bea promised me this would be an anonymous auction."

All Adam had to do was look at her and he would smile. She did that to him and he liked it. "I'll just have to sniff the air to know which one's yours." Adam didn't have to wait long before Khara's basket came up. He knew which basket was hers because his mother reminded him to tell Khara to put the pink ribbon on it, and because John started to bid on it.

"Do I hear twenty-five," Sam Tucker said.

"Twenty-five," Adam hollered out, gaining a surprised look from Khara and an angry one from John.

"What are you doing, Adam?" John asked, his brows drawn together, his forehead wrinkled.

"I'm starved." Adam thought that sounded like a good excuse.

"Thirty," John shouted out.

Without waiting for the auctioneer Adam said, "Forty."

"Fifty."

"One hundred dollars," Adam said, staring at John.

John's face reddened his tanned skin. "Why are you doing this? You know Khara and I are seeing each other."

"I'm hungry and I know Khara's basket's going to have good food in it." He could tell John didn't believe him.

John didn't take his eyes off of Adam when he shouted out, "One thousand dollars!"

Gasping could be heard throughout the crowd, then a hush rushed over the room. Adam knew John was testing him. If he raised the bid it would mean he wanted more than Khara's basket and Adam knew he wasn't ready to admit that to himself, let alone the entire town. The gavel smacked down on the podium, like a final sentencing, and echoed in his ears. John won. Adam watched his best friend and Khara walk up near the podium, get and pay for the basket, then go to the tables in the adjoining room.

Adam not only felt disappointed, he felt angry with himself. What would be so wrong with showing that he was interested in Khara? He'd never had that problem with other women before. But this time it was different. He thought of Khara in ways he'd never thought of a woman before. He could see himself marrying her and having children with her. That thought alone frightened him.

His glance remained on the doorway

Khara and John had walked through. Adam realized that if he didn't do something soon he'd probably lose her forever. That thought was worse than any fears he might have about marriage.

Adam bid on the next basket and won. As he walked up to pay for it, he noticed the frown on his mother's face. He wasn't sure why she looked so unhappy. Heck, didn't he do as she asked and bid on a young woman's basket — an *available* young woman? Sara Brown was a pretty blond that had in the past hinted to Adam that she was interested in him, but she was also only eighteen years old and looked twenty-five.

Sara selected a table away from Khara and John but in full view of them. Adam quickly held a chair out for Sara, then claimed the other seat that faced Khara and John.

"I just broke up with Roger," Sara said. "Boy, is he going to be jealous you bought my basket."

Adam vaguely heard what she'd said. He was too busy watching Khara and John laughing. John was sure putting on the charm. A surge of anger filled him.

"I'll unpack the basket." Sara lifted several items out.

It only took Adam one bite of greasy fried chicken before he knew he wasn't eating Khara's cooking. He hadn't realized until now how spoiled he'd become. Macaroni and cheese used to be a luxury. Now he only wanted Khara's meals. When had his palate changed?

Sara rambled on about her relationship with Roger, but Adam didn't hear a word of it, despite his occasional glances and nods at Sara.

"What is so interesting behind me?" Sara finally asked.

Adam's heart began to thump in his chest. He put on an easy smile. "Nothing. Why?"

"Because you keep staring over there." She looked over her shoulder, then turned back to him. "Is it that woman over there?" She tilted her head and long soft curls of hair drooped over her shoulder. "You're in love with her, aren't you?"

Adam laughed, despite the caution he felt inside. The last thing he wanted was the town to know his feelings toward Khara before he could tell or show her — or even figure them out for himself. "Of course not."

"Yes, you are. I can tell." She looked again. "Who is she?"

"Nobody. Now you were telling me about Roger?" His comment quickly changed Sara's thoughts and she continued to babble on.

Several times throughout the meal Adam had met Khara's glance. A bit of satisfaction swept through him when she looked at Sara and didn't appear happy. By the end of the day Adam decided he would have to somehow show Khara he cared about her.

Or it would be too late.

"Oh, great," Khara said on a groan as she hung up the phone on Adam's desk.

"What's wrong?" Adam asked, looking up from reading a contract.

"The woman from the Grange who was supposed to help me take a group of kids on an outing to the zoo just called and canceled. I don't know what I'm going to do." She lifted her shoulders in a shrug. "I can't go by myself."

Adam had been looking for just the right way to show Khara he cared about her and now the opportunity had just dropped in his lap. "I'll go with you."

After the moment of shock faded from Khara's face, she laughed. "I don't know, Adam. You and ten five-year-olds? You think you're up to it?"

Now it was Adam's turn to laugh. "Of course. I run a million-dollar business. How hard can ten five-year-olds be?"

"I didn't think you even liked children."

Adam felt slightly offended by her comment. Never once had he shown her he didn't like children. "I like kids. Heck, I used to be one."

"We wouldn't be keeping you from your work?"

She was giving him a gracious way of backing out, but Adam didn't want to back out. The idea of being with Khara all day long appealed to him, even if it was with a bunch of children. John was swamped with a big construction contract that would take him weeks to finish. During that time, Adam planned on taking advantage of John's absence. All was fair in love and war.

He held up his finger as he picked up the phone and dialed. "Hello, Mom. Something's come up and I won't be able to fix your leaky faucet today."

"I suppose it's that business of yours," Dolores said.

Adam could tell by the tone of his mother's voice that she was angry. He really couldn't blame her. He'd promised to fix that leak well over a month ago. But,

Adam suspected, his mother would be more than willing to put up with a leaky faucet for one more day if he was going out with a woman. It never mattered which woman he dated either. As far as his mother was concerned, any woman of childbearing years would do.

"No, it's not my business. Khara needs my help taking a group of kids to the zoo."

A dead silence hung over the phone before Dolores said, "That's a wonderful idea! I know you'll just love being around children. And Khara is such a darling young lady."

Adam cut his mother off, saying, "Got to go. Khara's waiting." If he'd hung on the phone any longer his mother would have started that same lecture on the necessity of getting married. And he'd heard that one too many times.

He got up from his chair and stepped around the desk. Making a sweeping gesture toward the door, he said, "Shall we go?"

Khara smiled and led the way into the garage. "I've borrowed a van from Sam Tucker. I'm supposed to pick it up at the Grange." She opened the garage door. "We'll take my car. I don't think I want to ride in your company vehicle again."

Adam laughed, the incident still fresh in his mind of Khara struggling to climb into the cab in her skirt and jacket. "It got you there, didn't it?"

"Yeah, well, I didn't get the job." The disappointment could be heard in her voice.

"How do you know that?"

"They would have called by now."

Adam opened the passenger door of her car and sat down. "I wouldn't give up so soon."

As if she didn't want to talk about it any-more, Khara turned the subject to the children. She told Adam the "do's and don'ts" of what to say and how to act. A couple of the children were on the hyperactive side and would take the most amount of work to keep track of.

They didn't have to wait long at the Grange before all ten of the children showed up. While Khara talked to the parents Adam struggled to round the children up as they played tag and elected him as "it." When he wouldn't cooperate and play with them one of the boys grabbed the sunglasses off his face and ran off with them.

Between the hot, sunny morning, and chasing the children, Adam had sweat dripping down the sides of his face by the time Khara said good-bye to the last parent and joined him.

He was exhausted and they hadn't even left yet.

"Okay, Jonathan," Khara said. "If you don't behave you won't be able to come with us. Now give Mr. Mansfield his glasses back."

Jonathan made a face and reluctantly handed them over. Adam stared at her in amazement. He'd issued that very same threat, but the little boy had ignored him. So how did Khara get Jonathan to listen to her?

"Okay, kids, let's get in the van," Adam said. He waved his hand and one by one he and Khara loaded them in and buckled them up. "I'll drive," he said as the last child's buckle snapped together. He'd rather drive the van than be put in charge of ten kids who wouldn't listen to a word he said.

The drive would take over two hours each way to get to the nearest zoo. At the rate these kids were bouncing in their seats, they would be tired before they reached their destination, which was fine with Adam. Keeping up with these little children would take all the energy he had.

Khara settled the children down by giving them books and pictures to color. Adam found himself constantly looking over at her. He couldn't stop himself from stealing glimpses despite his efforts. Something about her drew him like a magnet. He wished he could figure out how to break the attraction.

"Do you do this very often?" Adam asked, wanting to know more about her, all about her.

"Once in a while, but usually through work."

"So how'd you get roped into doing this?" He was doing it again — staring.

"I wouldn't say I was roped into it. Aunt Bea told me about a few of the families who couldn't afford to take their children many places and I offered to take them to the zoo." She shrugged.

"Do you think that's wise, using your own money?"

She narrowed her stare at him. "What do you mean?"

"Well, you should save your money for your house."

Khara folded her arms over her chest, her mouth turned down in a frown. "You mean to move it off your land." A child in the back started to cry and Khara turned her attention to her.

Grateful for the distraction, Adam searched his mind for a better topic. This conversation was not going well. His good intentions always seemed to come out wrong the minute he opened his mouth. He was concerned she would spend her money on these children instead of on food or bills. This need to protect her kept getting him into trouble. Adam decided he'd be better off keeping his mouth shut. So the remainder of the drive to the zoo was a quiet one.

As they pulled into a parking lot the children became excited, talking, laughing, screaming. Unloading the children turned out to be much easier than loading them had been. Khara pinned color-coded name tags on each child along with matching baseball caps with the Grange's insignia on them.

Since the zoo was on a hillside, they started at the bottom of the hill, where the Beluga whales were, and worked their way upward. Khara assigned the boys to Adam and she would take the girls. Adam thought he had gotten the short end of the deal, but understood the reasons why.

They didn't get far past the whales exhibit before several of the children had to go to the bathroom. Adam took the five boys in the men's room and waited while they used the facility.

"Mr. Mansfield," Tyler said in a whiny voice, "my shoe's untied."

Adam motioned the child over near the sink where the other boys were washing their hands, crouched down, and tied Tyler's shoe. Without warning, a splash of water struck Adam in the back. The boys roared in laughter. Adam stood, but before he could open his mouth Jonathan shot the cold water down the front of Adam's shirt and pants.

In one swift move Adam gripped Jonathan by the hand, leaned over, and glared into the child's face, the boy's smile fading to a fearful frown. "Either you behave or holding my hand will become permanent for the day." Adam hoped his glare was convincing. When Jonathan didn't reply Adam said, "Well? What'll it be?"

With a sharp jerk of the head Jonathan nodded and said, "I'll be good."

"Good." Looking at the other boys he said, "Let's go." As they exited the bathroom Adam found Khara and the girls waiting for them.

Her eyes flew to his shirt and pants, then widened. "Looks like you had some trouble." She tried to suppress a giggle, but did a poor job of it.

"Yeah, well, it won't happen again. Right, Jonathan?" Adam said.

"Right," Jonathan answered on a groan.

Khara opened her mouth to question him, but before she could say anything one of the girls tugged on her arm. "Let's go see the wolves."

As she passed by Adam she said, "At least the water will cool you down."

Adam wasn't sure if she meant cool his temper down or cool him from the heat. It must have been near eighty degrees by now. She was wrong on both accounts. The only thing he needed cooling down from was her.

"Mr. Mansfield, are we going to go?" Jonathan asked, his face scrunched with impatience, his small hand wedged in Adam's.

Adam glanced at the boy, then realized he'd been staring at Khara as she walked away. He couldn't help it. It was a natural reaction, or at least he hoped to convince himself it was. Giving in to Jonathan's demand, he followed at the end of the group. He figured that way he could at least keep his eyes on all five boys — and Khara — all at the same time.

They looked at a few more animals before many of the children complained about being hungry, conveniently while they were near a hot dog stand. "How would you kids like a hot dog and soda?" All ten children jumped for joy.

"Adam, I don't think that's a good idea. I have their lunches in the backpack," Khara said.

"Please, please, please," Amy, a pretty little girl with big blue eyes, said in a pleading tone as she stared up at Adam.

Adam glanced between Khara and Amy. He didn't want to undermine Khara's decision, but he couldn't disappoint Amy and the other children when he'd already promised them. He lifted his shoulders in a shrug. "Sorry," he said to Khara. "Next time I'll ask you first."

She raised her brows and smiled.

Like a cloud of locusts the children gathered around Adam as he bought the hot dogs and soda and handed them out. The boys scarfed their food down as if they hadn't eaten in weeks while the girls ate slowly and daintily as if they were at a tea party.

Jonathan sat down next to Adam, having suddenly become his bosom buddy. Adam could feel the boy staring at him while he ate. Just as Adam was about to take a bite of his hot dog Jonathan said, "Why do you have such big ears?"

Adam set his hot dog down, a little surprised by the question and unsure how to answer. When he looked at Khara she glanced away, laughing. He shrugged. "It's just the way I was made."

"Will I get big ears?"

"Probably."

As if the matter was settled, Jonathan finished his food, jumped up, and played tag with a few of the other boys. A warmth rushed through Adam as Khara scooted closer to him. "You gotta love him," she said.

"Yeah. I want ten more just like him," Adam said sarcastically.

Khara laughed, then quickly sobered. "Someday, when you meet the right person, you'll think differently about having children."

Adam glanced away, afraid she might see into his heart, into his soul. The thought of having children with Khara had already crossed his mind, more than once. He'd never even considered that option before with any other woman, even Pamela. What kind of father he would be like, he wasn't sure, but he knew one thing, that Khara would make an excellent mother. And that knowledge was important to him. He didn't want his children to have an over-bearing mother like he'd had. Above all, he didn't want a domineering wife. He wanted a woman who would be his equal, who would share the decisions in the family, a woman who would balance his own weaknesses with her strengths and vice versa.

"Mr. Mansfield," Jonathan said, "Kyle needs a handkerchief. He sneezed all over his clothes."

Adam hurried over to Kyle and cleaned him up. This was the first time he'd been around children for any length of time and was amazed at how demanding they were. His respect seemed to grow by leaps and bounds for Khara. He wondered how she did this on a daily basis — and liked it.

Adam rounded up the boys, wishing he had leashes for each one of them. Either that or tranquilizers. He returned to Khara and the girls, who were sitting quietly while they ate, talking about girlish stuff. Most definitely, he'd been given the harder group to contend with. "Shall we go see the elephants?"

After the children tossed their napkins and cups in the trash can, they led the way up the path to the elephant pen. "I can't see," Amy said, tugging on Adam's pant leg.

He glanced over at Khara and saw that she already had a child in her arms. He hoisted Amy up on his shoulders. She screamed with delight and clutched onto his hair, pulling it tight as if it was her only lifeline. He winced at the pain, which quickly subsided when Amy wrapped her arms around his head, her catsup-stained fingers pressing on one eye.

"Can you see the elephants?" Adam asked, moving her hand and sticky fingers.

Excitedly, Amy kicked her feet into his chest. He steadied them, then made his way to where Khara stood. She looked so natural with a child on her hip. "I want to see, too!" another child cried. One by one Adam hoisted each little girl on his shoulders so they could get a better look at the elephants. As he lifted down the last one, Cassie said, "I want cotton candy. It's right over there. Please, Mr. Mansfield. Please. I've never had it before." She pointed and tugged on Adam's shirt to make sure she had his full attention.

He glanced at Khara for her approval but she only shrugged, leaving him to decide. What harm could it do? Like shadows, all ten children followed him to the stand and waited impatiently for their cone of cotton candy. Of course, the boys wanted blue and the girls wanted pink.

Their next stop was the aquarium where they saw many varieties of fish in one large tank. In smaller viewing windows displays of jellyfish floated in the water, their tentacles spread, looking like parachutes, and starfish of all sizes along with more tropical fish of brilliant blue, yellow, red, and black. The sharks were in a separate building, and afterward the children wanted popcorn. This time Khara objected.

"Let them live a little," Adam said. He could easily afford something these children considered a luxury.

"Please!" the children cried in unison, now surrounding Khara.

She laughed. "It looks like I'm outnumbered." She lifted her hands in surrender. "Okay, but no more after this."

The children all agreed. The group looked at several more exhibits and played on the grassy knolls before they decided to call it a day. Just as they reached the exit gate Amy pulled on Adam's sleeve. "I don't feel so good, Mr. Mansfield."

Just as he bent down to ask her what was wrong, Amy threw up on his shoe. For a moment all Adam could do was stand there and stare in shock. He looked over at Khara. She pointed toward the bathroom, the expression on her face shouting I-told-you-so. With a stiff leg Adam hobbled into the bathroom and cleaned up while Khara took care of Amy in the girls' bathroom.

Definitely, he was glad to be leaving. Running ten miles would have been easier. He'd hoped to spend time with Khara today. In fact, that's why he offered to go with her. To impress her. Instead, children asked him questions, sprayed him with water, sat on his shoulders, smeared catsup on his face, and threw up on his shoe. He doubted he'd impressed Khara. Usually he felt in control, but today the children had controlled him, and had monopolized Khara's attention and time.

The only way he'd be able to have time with her was if he asked her out on a date, but how could he do that now that she was seeing John? Especially when he so vehemently denied that he had any interest in Khara to all his poker buddies. No, for now he'd have to settle for seeing her at the house. He had to remember he was a confirmed bachelor. And that's the way he should stay if he knew what was good for him.

★ ★ ★

"Dolores, I feel ridiculous in this getup. We're wearing overcoats and hats in eighty-degree weather!" Bea said.

"You don't want Khara and Adam to know we're here at the zoo spying on them, do you?"

"No."

"Then stop complaining." Dolores put her sunglasses back on.

Bea folded her arms over her chest and glanced away when a person passing by gave them a strange look. "I don't know why we're here, anyway."

"Because," Dolores said, "when I heard my son was coming here to help Khara out with ten children I had to see it for myself to believe it. He must be interested in her to do this. Adam's never shown any interest in children before. Just look at him. He's a natural with them. Maybe they'll have children right away." She clapped her hands together. "Wouldn't that be wonderful? Our dream will finally have come true."

"*Our* dream?" Bea planted her hands on her hips.

Dolores looked at her and made a face. "You want grandchildren, too."

"I'm Khara's aunt. They wouldn't be my grandchildren."

133

"Close enough." Dolores grasped Bea's arm and whispered, "They're coming our way. Quick. Hide behind these bushes!" They scurried behind a big rhododendron. As Khara, Adam, and the children walked by, Dolores said, "Look the other way."

A few seconds later Bea said, "They're gone." She groaned. "I'm hot and tired. I need a lemonade."

"Is that all you ever think about? We need to follow them."

"Why? We know they're going to look at more animals."

A long sigh escaped Dolores's mouth. "I suppose you're right. Our plan is working. Now we have to somehow get Adam thinking in terms of marriage." She squinted her eyes in thought and tapped her index finger on her cheek.

"Come on. Let's go home." Bea led the way around the corner, then halted when they spotted the group over at the elephants.

"Look how close Adam's standing next to Khara," Dolores said, a wide smile deepening the grooves at the corners of her mouth. She lifted her hand and Bea met it, giving her a high five, knowing their plan was indeed working.

★ ★ ★

After Khara and Adam dropped the children and the van off they drove home. Adam was exhausted. He headed straight for the couch and plopped on it. Working outside all day long didn't exhaust him as much as ten children had. How did Khara manage to work with kids on a daily basis? He didn't have the patience or the energy, yet she remained calm no matter what they did. In fact the only time he could remember her getting upset was with him. Should he be flattered or insulted?

The phone rang on his desk and he just stared at it. Khara hurried in from the kitchen and answered it, giving him an exasperated glance. "Just a minute," she said, and stretched the phone over to him.

"Where the heck have you been?" Dan, an employee of his, said. "We've been trying to get a hold of you all day."

"I've been out. What's up?"

"We've had an accident. One of the rollers broke."

Adam cursed under his breath and pushed to a sitting position. "That'll delay the job."

"I know."

"Does it look like someone messed with it?"

Dan hesitated. "Yes."

"I'll be there as soon as possible." Feeling more tired than he had in years, Adam hung up the phone. He thought he could find the culprit by staying at Khara's and watching, but that was proving unsuccessful. When he found out who was doing this to him, there would be a price to pay. "I won't be home for dinner. We've got a problem at the site."

Khara frowned with concern, but only said, "Okay."

As Adam headed out the door a warmth spread through him. She cared about him. She really cared.

Chapter Seven

Khara enjoyed working with Taylor. Without his handicap, the boy would probably be the smartest student in class. She had made real progress with him, and did not look forward to the end of summer, when Taylor would return to school and no longer use her services.

"We're through with the lesson," Khara said.

Taylor smiled and signed, "Okay."

They walked together out the front door to wait for his mother. Adam stood out there talking to one of his employees, Dan. He glanced in Khara's direction, met her smile, then turned back to Dan.

"I was hoping to send you home with one of those cookies we made today," Khara said. "But they're not done yet."

A disappointed expression crossed Taylor's face. He dipped his chin. The buzzer on the stove rang, brightening his eyes.

Khara held her finger up. "Adam, would you watch Taylor for a minute while I get the cookies out of the oven?"

Adam gave a quick nod in her direction.

Khara hurried into the kitchen, removed the tray, and placed the cookies on the cooling rack. She grabbed several paper towels and placed a couple of cookies in them. She heard the sound of the hauling trucks returning from an early morning job. After weeks of hearing them, she was finally beginning to get used to the screeching of their brakes and the deep roar of their engines. She hurried back outside. When she stepped onto the porch and didn't see Taylor anywhere, a swell of panic filled her.

"Adam, where's Taylor?"

Adam glanced over at her, his brows drawing together as if he didn't know what she was talking about.

"I asked you to watch . . . oh, no, Taylor!" Khara pointed to the little boy, playing in the driveway, right in the way of the oncoming truck.

Adam rushed into action, racing across the yard, his long legs covering the ground in huge leaps. The man driving the logging truck saw the little boy. The brakes screeched at the sudden change in motion.

Khara stood there, frozen to the ground in fear. She could hardly breathe. As badly as she wanted to look away, she watched and prayed for Adam to reach Taylor in time.

Just at the last second, Adam scooped the child into his arms and dove to one side of the driveway, rolling over with Taylor nestled in his arms. The truck lurched to a stop several feet past where Taylor had been playing.

Taylor laughed as if he thought he was playing a game. Adam stood, blood dripping from an abrasion on his arm, yet he ignored it. Khara saw distress in Adam's eyes.

Her heart pounded, vibrating every limb. Her body felt suddenly weak with relief, but anger quickly renewed her strength. As Adam and Taylor reached her she said, "You were supposed to be watching him. This is all your fault. If you weren't living here this would never have happened."

Adam's eyes hardened. In a low, controlled tone he said, "You should have watched him then."

"But you promised to watch him for me." She pulled Taylor to her and rested her hands on his shoulders.

"I didn't hear what you said. I was talking to Dan."

"You nodded like you'd heard me."

He raised his hands in the air and let

them smack to his side. "I'm trying to run a business here."

"And you don't have two minutes to watch Taylor for me?"

"He's your responsibility."

"Gee," Dan said, interrupting them, "if I didn't know any better I would think you two were married and talking about your own child."

Khara opened her mouth to argue more with Adam, then stopped as Dan's words sunk in. Heat rose in her cheeks. They did sound like a married couple. The thought sent excitement and fear shooting through her at the same time. The idea of being married to Adam sounded so right, seemed so right, yet it wasn't what she wanted.

Adam would only leave her in the end. Everyone else had. Her parents, her best girlfriend, and Joel, her boyfriend of two years. Within a year's time everyone close to her, everyone she had depended upon, left her. The phone calls had stopped a long time ago, along with the occasional letter. About the same time as when Khara had decided to go it alone — forever.

Day after day, she felt herself depending on Adam. The longer they lived together the more she looked forward to seeing him in the morning, busy working at his desk. Talking with him over meals. He'd helped her out with the house, too, painting, roofing, and doing general maintenance. He'd even bulldozed and tilled an area for a garden and promised that it wasn't too late in the summer for her to grow green beans, lettuce, and carrots.

When Khara glanced at Adam she noticed he, too, had a redness to his cheeks. He hesitated before he said, "Look, I'm sorry."

In a quiet voice Khara said, "I'm sorry too."

The uncomfortable moment was broken as Taylor's mother drove up. Taylor ran over to her and jumped in the car. They both waved good-bye as the car pulled away. Taylor's mother wasn't much for conversation, not even when it concerned her son. Khara had to call her at home just to give her an update of his progress.

Khara returned to the kitchen and placed more dough on the cookie sheet. Just as she slid it into the oven the phone rang.

"This is Kevin Sutton from the school. I'd like to see you today if I could."

Khara's pulse quickened. "Is this about the job?"

"Yes. Can you meet me at the school in about an hour?"

"Yes." Her answer came swiftly.

"Good. See you there."

She held the phone to her chest and closed her eyes, praying she got the job. It would mean the difference between keeping her house, or moving back to Seattle. She had given up a lot to move to Morton: a secure job, an apartment she'd been comfortable in, and good pay. Bea was that important to her, and Khara knew what it was like to be alone. The last thing she wanted was for Bea to have to spend the last years of her life without family around. Khara longed for family. She envied the large families with lots of children. How many times had she wished for brothers and sisters? Too many to count. Bea had always been there for her, helping her out with money for college, someone to talk to. Now that Bea needed Khara, she intended to return the favor, return the love, return the concern and care.

Hurrying into her bedroom, she changed into a skirt, blouse, and heels, brushed her hair out, and returned to the kitchen to find Adam in there. "I took the cookies out of the oven."

"Thanks."

"What are you all dressed up for?"

Khara didn't want to tell him about the job until she knew for sure if she got it. Kevin Sutton could just want to clarify some details on her application, or possibly set up a second interview. Whatever the case, she didn't want to say anything until she knew for sure what he wanted. "I have to run into town and meet with someone. Could you turn the stove off for me, please? I'll finish the cookies later."

"Are you meeting John?" His tone sounded accusing, as if she was doing something wrong.

"No."

As she hurried into the garage she heard him say, "Will you be home for dinner?"

Khara didn't answer. She didn't have time. She wanted to get to the school and find out what Kevin wanted — and see if she got the job. Jumping in her car, she revved the engine and shifted into reverse. She didn't bother shutting the garage door as she sped out of the driveway and into town.

As she waited at the red light, she tapped her finger on the steering wheel, every muscle in her body tense. If she got this job it would not only mean she could re-main in a career she loved, but she could afford to fix her house up — and possibly hire a lawyer to get Adam out of her life.

That thought sent her heart plummeting. She struggled to suppress the feeling.

The light changed to green and she pressed on the gas. Adam couldn't remain in her life. He had caused nothing but trouble from the day he'd moved in. He'd disrupted her life in more ways than she could count. Many times, she suspected, had been deliberate. As long as she lived she couldn't forget how he'd forced his way into her life and into her home, threatening to make her move her house.

She pulled into the entrance to the elementary school and parked out front. Her heart began to race again as she got out of the car and made her way to the front door. Her palms moistened when she spotted Kevin waiting there to greet her.

He extended his hand. "I'm glad you could make it." He motioned for her to follow him into an office where he sat behind the desk. "Please, sit down."

"Do you have more questions?" Khara asked, hoping she sounded calm.

"Only one." Kevin smiled. "Would you be interested in accepting the job?"

Emotion filled Khara's throat. She felt like crying with relief. Quickly, she composed herself and returned an easy smile. "I'd love to."

"Good. I need you to fill out a few forms, which you can take home and read." He slid the forms in an envelope and set them at the edge of the desk. "Right now, I'd like to show you your new classroom." He rose and led the way through the hall, stopping at an open door.

Khara peeked inside. Decorating possibilities flowed through her mind. She stepped through the doorway and further into the room. One corner she would use for the children to paint on easels. Another she would use for a play corner where the children could build things out of blocks and put giant puzzles together. She pictured one wall, near the door, where she would set up a weather scene and each day the children could learn about the weather by putting up clouds, sun, or raindrops.

Bringing her out of her thoughts Kevin said, "I hadn't intended to hire you. I thought you would want too much pay, considering your experience. But after Adam called me and told me how good you were with children . . ." Kevin bobbed his head. "I couldn't pass up someone with your talent. I figured you'd be worth the extra pay."

Khara whirled around. "Adam called you?"

"Yeah." Kevin grinned. "I've known him and his family for years. He felt bad about interrupting your interview and asked me to give you another chance. We got to talking about you, and he told me how you tutor children in your home. He said a lot of very nice things about you. I'm looking forward to having someone as dedicated as you are on my staff."

"I'm looking forward to working here," Khara said. Her excitement soared as they left the classroom and returned to Kevin's office. She thanked him and headed out the door, feeling as if she was floating on a cloud. As she got in her car, started it up, and drove away, her thoughts remained on Adam. He'd called even after she had ordered him not to. She'd even demanded he stay out of her life. Now if it weren't for him, she wouldn't have gotten the job, and at the same pay that she made at her old job in Seattle. She had expected a huge pay cut, and she would have taken it, too.

Maybe she had misjudged Adam. For the first time she could be truly thankful he *had* moved into the house and into her life. Somehow she would have to repay him for calling Kevin, but how?

As she pulled into the garage and entered the house she found Adam working at his desk. She struggled to suppress the urge to rush over to him and give him a big kiss — on the lips. One thing she couldn't hold back was her smile. She cleared her throat to gain his attention.

When he glanced over at her his eyes widened. "Don't you look like the cat that ate the canary."

"Thank you, Adam."

He tilted his head and drew his brows together, then came around the front of his desk, sat on the edge, and folded his arms over his chest. "For what?"

"For calling Kevin Sutton. I got the job." She couldn't have stopped herself if she had wanted to. And right now she didn't want to as she stepped forward and kissed him on the cheek. "If it weren't for you I wouldn't have."

He stood to his full height, his eyes taking on a hazy glaze, his voice slightly husky. "I'm glad I could help."

A moment of awkwardness followed. Khara didn't know what else to say, and the way he looked at her made her lose all logical thought. "Well, I, uh, should get dinner started." Khara turned, but before she could take a step Adam reached out and grabbed her. In one swift move, she found herself gathered in his arms.

Adam gazed at her before his mouth came down on hers, first in hungry demand, then lightening to a softer, more tender kiss.

Khara felt dizzy. She let the kiss linger until he broke it, lifting his head. Struggling for her voice she said, "I guess I owe you one."

Adam lifted his brows, but didn't loosen his hold. "And I know just how you could pay me back."

"How?" Her question came out on a whisper.

"You could settle our land dispute by selling me the house."

Chapter Eight

Khara's entire body stiffened. She stared at him in disbelief. Did he really say what she thought she'd heard him say? Pushing out of his arms, she took several steps back to distance herself from him and his hurtful words. Her heart felt as if he'd just trampled it. How could he suggest such a thing? Anger filled every fiber in her and reddened her face as she glared at him.

"Sell you my house?"

Adam's forehead wrinkled, and again, he tilted his head to one side as if he didn't understand her mood.

"And where would I live?" Khara asked, spitting each word out, her hands fisted at her sides.

"Here, of course. I'd lease the house to you. I have no need for it."

Each word fueled her temper. He would buy her house, probably for dirt cheap, then rent it to her. Of all the nerve. Adam Mansfield had just pushed her too far. She refused to take this, or anything else he intended to dish out, any longer. She would rid herself of this man once and for all — even if it was the last thing she would ever do.

Too angry to speak, Khara spun on her heels, stormed out of the room, and entered her bedroom, shutting her door with extra oomph. With her arms folded over her chest, she paced at the base of her bed. How could she get Adam out of her life? First she would have to get him out of her house. How?

Khara already knew the answer to her question: a lawyer, one outside of this town who didn't know Adam. The town of Morton was too close-knit. Everyone knew Adam and liked him, except for her. She had seen a side of Adam that many hadn't. And he'd shown that side one too many times for Khara's liking.

The back door shut, drawing her out of her thoughts. She peeked out her bedroom window and spotted Adam rounding the house, undoubtedly to get in his truck. Good. Perfect. He was leaving. This would give her the opportunity to call a lawyer and set up an appointment. She stalked to the kitchen and whipped open a phone book and turned to the attorney section in the yellow pages. She selected one and dialed. Luckily, he had an opening the next morning.

As Khara hung up the phone, she wondered if she'd done the right thing, then Adam's words came rushing back, renewing her determination to get him out of her life.

Adam set the table while Khara finished making the hamburgers. The tension still lingered between them, the dispute over the house still fresh in their minds.

"Don't you want to eat at the counter?" Khara asked.

"No. I want to be able to look at you when we talk." He placed a plate at each spot. The phone rang. Adam quickly picked it up.

"Adam. It's Dan. I'm calling from my car. I was driving by the shed and saw someone snooping around. You might want to check it out."

A whisper of a curse crossed his lips before he hung the phone up.

Khara frowned. "What's wrong?"

"Nothing. I'll be back in a minute." Adam disappeared out the back door. The sun had started to set. The tall fir trees cast haunting shadows. Once the light slid behind the hill it would be dark and Adam would be out of luck.

Adam took off at a run. This was the

151

break he'd been waiting for. He still couldn't figure out who would want to hurt his business. Everyone in town was his friend. The bigger question than who was why? Why would someone do this?

As he rounded a clump of trees he spotted the suspect inside the fence, his head bent toward the engine of the dozer. Adam stepped carefully, stealthily, creeping closer. Rounding to the front, he blocked the only exit. A truck with an empty loader stood between Adam and the culprit, but Adam couldn't see his face, only the broad shoulders covered in a worn brown jacket.

"Having problems with my dozer?" Adam said.

The man froze.

Adam took a step. He could tell the saboteur couldn't decide what to do. Then like a gazelle running through tall prairie grass, the man took off, sprinting to the back fence. In one giant leap, he hopped the fence.

On a run, Adam flew out the exit, rounding the shed, but by the time he reached the back, the man had climbed over and was running toward the cabin. Adam pursued. By the time he reached the front of the house, he was breathing heavily. The front door stood ajar.

Adam plunged forward. He paused in the foyer, listening for any noise. A loud thud, followed by a grunt, sounded at the back of the house. The culprit made the wrong turn, and cornered himself in a room with no windows. Adam blocked the door.

"I think we've had enough cat-and-mouse chase," Adam said, flipping on a light.

The man's shoulders slumped. Slowly, he stood and pivoted.

Adam sucked in a breath. "John?" He could barely say his name. "Why?"

John hung his head. "I don't know. I — I haven't been able to keep up with you and your bids. I — I guess I just couldn't lose to you."

They had always been competitive, but to Adam it had been in fun, in perspective. He'd lost contracts to John many times in the past, yet never once had he considered sabotaging John's equipment and business.

"First it was about business," John said. "Then there was Khara . . ."

"What about Khara?" Adam sounded defensive, felt defensive. He didn't care.

"Come on, Adam. I can see the way you look at each other."

Was he that transparent?

John continued, "I've never been able to compete with you on an equal playing field."

"What did it matter, John?"

"It mattered to me. I hate losing. Especially to you. You were always the best in school, at sports, at everything we did."

Adam felt as if a knife had just stabbed him in the gut. He'd known John since childhood. He'd considered him his best friend. How could he have misjudged him so badly?

"Adam?" Khara said from the entryway.

Adam met John's stare. "Are you going to tell her?" John asked.

"No," Adam said. "You are."

After John left, Khara and Adam remained unmoving, an awkward silence hanging between them.

"I'm sorry," Khara whispered.

Adam shrugged. "At least the problems will stop now."

Khara forced a smile. She knew he had to be hurting, but he did his best to hide his feelings, his emotions. Wanting to help him get his mind off the sore subject of John, she gazed around the cabin. "Wow. I didn't expect the cabin to be so far along."

"Would you like to see the rest of it?"

She nodded. She expected to see a one- or two-room cabin like the kind the pioneers had built. Instead the home stood two stories and extended out on both sides of the front porch. Inside a huge rock fireplace caught her eye and seemed to be the focal point of the living room. Huge windows allowed light into the rooms. Looking out the front window, Adam had his own private lake. Beyond that was a meadow, then the woods. The mountains stood out in the distance, making the view spectacular, the sun a sparkling diamond on the horizon.

Adam stood behind her, rested one hand on her shoulder, and pointed with the other. "I'm having my shop built way over there by those groups of trees."

His breath brushed her cheek, stirring strands of her hair. His lips remained near her ear for a moment before he straightened. A tingling sensation ran through Khara. She had never reacted to a man the way she did with Adam. Her attraction to him seemed to have no bounds. The heat from him warmed her and she missed it, longed for it, the moment he stepped away.

He continued their tour and showed her the five bedrooms, four baths, two fireplaces, three balconies, a huge kitchen (which Khara liked the best), and a wine cellar, along with the massive living room and sunroom. The formal dining room floor was made of marble and could easily fit a table seated for twelve. "I'm also having a three-car garage built." He took her by the hand and led her up to a loft that technically would be considered a third floor.

"What are you going to use this room for?" she asked.

"A playroom. I hope to fill the house with a wife and children someday soon."

She glanced over her shoulder at him and their eyes met. As his head bent forward she held her breath. She wasn't sure she wanted him to kiss her until their lips touched.

Then he spun her beyond time and space with each kiss, each gentle touch, each whispered word. Khara let herself relax. Every caress, every kiss took her from the strict, practical world she had created for herself. She had sought solitude for so long, thinking she needed her freedom, fearing abandonment. Now all she wanted was Adam.

His hair brushed against her cheek as his mouth returned to her neck. She closed her eyes, wanting to savor the feeling, the moment. A sense of rightness flowed into her, a sweet sensation. Only with Adam had she felt like this. Only with him did she realize her need to have someone in her life. Only with him would she try again.

He lifted his head and gazed at her as if trying to memorize every detail of her face. He traced his finger over her cheekbone, down along her jawline. Tenderly, he let his lips show her the words he hadn't yet spoken.

He lifted his head and in a hoarse voice said, "I love you. I've never needed anyone before, but I need you." Before he could claim her mouth once again they heard a car pull up to the front of the house, footsteps entered the cabin and climbed the stairs.

"Anyone here?" a voice yelled out.

Adam stepped to the staircase and looked down. "We're up here."

"I thought you might be here." A middle-aged man with thinning hair and glasses reached the top step. His glance met Adam's then rested on Khara. "I didn't mean to interrupt anything," he said.

"No, you didn't interrupt anything," Adam said, a little too quickly, a little too breathlessly. "I was just showing Khara the cabin." He added, "Khara, this is Tom Forth. He's the contractor building my house."

She nodded and smiled, then stepped to the window as the two men began to talk. She closed her eyes and let the breeze cool her down.

The realization suddenly hit. She was in love with Adam.

Khara couldn't remember the last time she'd fallen in love, and maybe she never really had. All she knew was that an elated feeling filled her and she wished it would never go away. She wanted a lasting relationship, but only with Adam. Wrapping her hands around her waist, she hugged herself. This time would this dream end happily ever after?

"Khara!" Adam yelled.

She could hear him from her bedroom loud and clear, and came running out. "What? What happened?"

Adam slammed a letter down on the kitchen counter. "Why didn't you just tell me? You made me go on like a fool, telling you I loved you. How could you lead me on like this?" His brows drew together, his lips curled in a sneer, his eyes filled with a combination of hurt, anger, and betrayal.

She shook her head and swallowed, almost afraid to find out what he was talking about. In a calm voice she said, "What happened, Adam?"

"Your lawyer is what happened. He put a lien on my log home. The contractor can't work on it until this land dispute is decided — again."

Khara picked the letter up, her hands shaking. She scanned the words that ordered Adam to move out of her house. "Adam . . . I —"

"Save it, Khara. I don't want to hear any more lies." He charged into the family room, grabbed a box out of the corner, and began to fill it with papers, file folders, and bills.

She followed him. Heat rose to her cheeks as anger built inside. She tried to keep her voice at a calm level, but failed. "You have some nerve getting mad at me about this. You're the one who barged into my life and told me — no, demanded — that I let you live in my house."

His hands froze and he glared at her. "If you didn't want me here you should have just said so."

She forced a laugh. "I did tell you a million times."

Adam started to pack again. "I thought you were different from other women. I shouldn't have trusted you."

"Look. I didn't know my lawyer was going to do this. I went to see him after you asked to buy my house. I was scared. I didn't know what else to do."

He hefted the box off the desk and charged down the hall. "Tell it to *my* lawyer."

She followed. "As usual, you're being impossible."

He halted at the front door, then whirled around to face her. "*I'm* being impossible? At least I'm open and honest with you. I didn't go behind your back and throw you off my land."

He reached for the door handle and turned it.

"Yes, you did. You took this land dispute to court before my aunt gave me the house. You did that on purpose because you knew you could win with her."

He narrowed his glare at her. "Don't twist this around. I'm not the manipulative one here. You are."

Khara pointed to the door. "Get out of my house and stay out."

"Gladly."

Khara breathed heavily as she watched

Adam storm to his car, passing Bea and Dolores on his way. When the two ladies reached the door their gray brows had drawn from confusion to worry.

"What's wrong with Adam?" Dolores said. "I've never seen him so upset."

Khara stepped aside for the two ladies to enter, then shut the door behind them. She expelled a deep sigh. "Adam asked me to sell him the house. I thought he was going to make me move the house if I didn't sell, so I talked to a lawyer." She led them into the kitchen and handed Bea the letter. "Adam received this in the mail today."

Khara walked to the refrigerator and lifted out a pitcher of iced tea. Reaching into the cupboard she pulled out three tall glasses and filled them with ice, tea, and a slice of lemon. She placed them on a tray along with a plate of cookies, carried them to the table, and sat down. Bea and Dolores followed, sitting across from her.

"I tried to tell Adam why I went to a lawyer, but he wouldn't listen to a word I said." She wrapped her paper napkin around her finger.

"Why would he have gotten so upset over that? I would have thought he would have expected you to ask a lawyer for advice. After all, your house is on his property," Bea said.

Khara hesitated a glance at them before staring into her cup. "Adam and I were becoming . . . close. He thinks I betrayed him." Heat rose in her cheeks as disappointment washed through her.

Bea and Dolores exchanged looks. "What do you mean, close?" Dolores asked as her penciled eyebrows rose.

Khara lifted her shoulders, then let them drop. "You know. We had feelings for each other."

Bea gasped. "You mean like boyfriend and girlfriend?"

"Yeah."

"What will you do now?" Bea asked.

"I don't know. I doubt Adam will ever talk to me again." Suddenly she felt like crying. She hadn't realized the ramifications of their fight until now. She blinked, struggling to keep tears from forming. With a lump in her throat she took a sip of her tea. The urge to bake came over her. She would try a French dish with a complicated sauce. That would relax her and ease her worries.

Bea patted her hand. "We're here for you, honey. We'll help you out any way we can."

"Oh, Aunt Bea," Khara said on a sigh. "I don't know what anyone could do. Maybe it's better this way. It seems like every relationship I get involved with goes sour." She shook her head. "Adam's so fickle. One day he shows me his house and tells me he intends to fill it with a wife and children soon, and the next he storms out and never wants to see me again."

"What?" Bea and Dolores said in unison, their eyes bulging wide.

"My son said that?"

Khara waved the comment off with a gesture of her hand. "No, it's over between Adam and me. Nothing could bring us back together."

"No. I won't hear of it," Dolores said. "We've worked too hard for this."

"What?" Khara frowned.

A thud sounded from under the table followed by Dolores crying, "Ouch."

"Never mind, honey," Bea said. "Dolores says things sometimes . . ." She circled her finger in the air by her head, then pointed to Dolores as if she was crazy.

Dolores rolled her eyes and looked away in disgust. "Just leave Adam to me. I'll take care of everything."

Khara wasn't sure what she meant. At the moment she didn't care. She would accept the fact that Adam was out of her life — somehow.

As Khara drove to Bea's for dinner she thought about Adam having come over to her house earlier that day. The tension had been so thick she could have sliced it with a dull knife from the second he'd walked in. He'd barely spoken a word the entire time he was there to pick up clothes and toiletries. And really, he hadn't needed to say anything because he'd said it all the day before.

Khara arrived at her aunt's apartment with a large bowl of salad in her hands. She only waited a second or two before Bea answered. The instant Khara stepped into the house she saw Adam and halted.

She'd been set up. By her sweet, dear aunt.

"What is he doing here?" Khara asked.

"What's she doing here?" Adam demanded. He stood. "If she's going to be here, then I'm leaving." He headed for the door.

Before his fingers wrapped around the handle Dolores said, "Hold it right there, Adam Mansfield. You sit yourself down on that couch right now."

Khara could hear him mutter under his

breath before he turned around and planted himself down.

"We thought the two of you could settle this matter if you'd just talk to each other," Dolores said.

Adam folded his arms over his chest. "There's nothing to talk about."

"Got that right." Khara dropped her purse on the nearest chair, walked from the room, into the kitchen, and plopped her salad on the counter. In a low whisper she said, "How could you do this to me?"

Bea rubbed her hands together. "We were only trying to help."

Khara expelled a breath. "I know." She wondered how she would ever get through this evening, because if looks could kill Adam would have shot her dead the moment she had walked in that door. Every time she thought about how he was mad at *her* an anger ignited inside. He started this whole situation, barging into her life, making threats, and causing havoc in her life. She refused to apologize for going to a lawyer to protect her rights and house.

"Why don't you go out there and talk to him?" Bea said pleadingly. When Khara didn't answer or budge she added, "You can't stay in the kitchen all night long."

Reluctantly Khara pivoted, took a deep

breath, and entered the living room. She almost laughed at the picture Adam made, sitting on the couch, his arms folded over his broad chest, his feet wide and planted firm to the rug, his expression unyielding. She selected a chair furthest from him and stiffly sat down.

He fixed his eyes on a lamp across the room and stared at it.

The room fell silent. Khara refused to initiate a conversation. He started this battle, and it was up to him to end it.

Dolores raised her hands in the air and let them flop to her side with a smack before she stormed into the kitchen.

After several minutes Adam said, "I suppose this was your idea?"

Khara folded her arms over her chest. "I was just about to ask you the very same question."

He glanced at her, then looked away as if the mere sight of her hurt his eyes. "I haven't told my men about . . . our situation, so the trucks and equipment will still be at your house."

She lifted her shoulders. "Take your time. I can always lease you the space."

He glared at her, anger seeping red up his neck. "I was doing you a favor, offering to buy that dump."

"It's not a dump."

"Oh, no? I had a new roof put on, I painted it for you, fixed the stove, among other things — and you have the nerve to put a lien on my log home for damages. You do realize that shut my contractor down?"

Khara looked away. She'd read the letter, but the only legal jargon she'd understood was the part that ordered Adam out of her house. This entire time she thought that's why he was so upset. Guilt started to seep in, yet she refused to apologize.

"It could take months before we go to court over the land," Adam said, then fell silent.

"It's time to eat," Bea said as she set a pork roast on the table.

Placed across the table from each other, Khara and Adam avoided looking at each other as much as possible. The tension grew as the minutes ticked off the grandfather clock, the click annoying and continuous. The only sound that could be heard around the table was the clinking of utensils, dishing food up or cutting on the plate, and an occasional sigh.

"This salad's sure good, Mother," Adam said.

"Khara made it."

"Oh."

Despite the knot in her stomach, Khara tried to force her food down. Once through the meal, Adam accidentally touched his foot with hers. Their glances met briefly, before he looked down at his plate. After the meal, Dolores sent them back into the living room, using the excuse of having to clean up as a reason to leave them alone.

Adam stood in the center of the room, his arms crossed over his chest and feet shoulder width apart. "I wish you'd come to your senses and just sell me the stupid house."

"Come to my senses," Khara stated, repeating his words to make sure she'd heard him right. "You're the one that's being unreasonable." She shook her head, too angry to even fight about it. "I'm leaving." She stood and picked up her purse.

"No. *I'm* leaving," Adam said.

They both rushed to exit. Adam got there first, whipping the door open, and grinning that he'd beat her. They both moved to the opening at the same time and collided.

"I was here first," Khara said.

"No, I was, but you go ahead." He made an exaggerated gesture for her to step through first as if bowing to royalty.

Khara flung her purse over her shoulder and almost hit Adam with it before she charged through the door. She hurried down the hall and out of the building, feeling Adam on her heels the entire way.

When she reached her car Adam grabbed her arm and spun her around. For each step he took toward her she backed up, bumping her backside into the car door. He advanced until his body nearly touched hers. He glared at her, his eyes filled with anger, along with something else.

"Sell me your house and I won't even charge you rent." His voice had become husky.

Khara's breath caught in her throat when his finger stroked her cheek. She swallowed. She turned around and struggled to get the key in the lock. When she finally did she yanked the door open, hitting him with it, slid into the seat, started the engine, and drove away. When she glanced in the rearview mirror she saw Adam standing there watching her.

So many emotions ran through Khara. She didn't know how to feel or what to think. What really bothered her was that he had the ability to hurt her. Isn't that what she'd protected herself from all these years? Isn't that why she'd given up on dating, given up on men? She shouldn't have let Adam into her life, and especially into her heart.

She drove for home, eventually puttering into the garage. When she entered her house, she automatically glanced at Adam's desk. She shut the door with a click that seemed to echo throughout the empty house. A lump formed in her throat. The quiet, the loneliness of the place, screamed out at her. Alone. Half of a whole. A part of her was missing. She wanted to talk to someone, but who? She had no idea where her parents were, she hadn't talked to her best friend in over a year, and Bea wouldn't be objective about her situation.

For the first time in two years Khara allowed herself to cry, allowed herself to feel pity. She wished school would start soon so she could dive into her work, get involved with her students — anything to take her mind off of Adam. For now, she would focus on Taylor and perhaps fix her house up. So many things needed to be repaired.

She gazed around the room. So many things were in dire need of repair. Adam was right. The place was a dump.

Chapter Nine

Adam searched the grounds for Khara. He wondered if she would come to the Logger's Jubilee, an annual event held in the summer. He'd entered several events, as he did every year, just for the fun of it. This year his mind wasn't on the competition, though. He scanned the crowd again wishing he could get her off of his mind and out of his dreams.

"Who are you looking for?" Tiffany asked.

Adam glanced at her, wondering why he'd asked her to go with him to this event. She was nice, but she wasn't Khara. How that woman had a hold on him! When they'd been at dinner, last week, all evening long he'd wanted to pull her into his arms and kiss her. He wasn't sure if he was fighting the land dispute or his feelings for her.

Tiffany slipped her hand through his arm and pulled him along. "Come on. There's the gang."

As she talked with her friends, Adam

glanced at Tiffany. No doubt about it, Tiffany had a beautiful face. Not too long ago, that would have been enough for him, but not any longer. He wanted more. He wanted to be able to have an intelligent conversation with his date. At twenty-two, Tiffany didn't have much in common with him. He used to be able to put up with idle chatter with his mind completely focused on a woman's beauty. What surprised him the most was that he wasn't turned on by Tiffany *because* her mind was so empty.

When had he changed?

He took a deep breath, expelled his frustration, then scanned the crowd again. Khara's red hair flashed out at him. His pulse increased.

It amazed him how the mere sight of her could affect him. But what he missed most was their conversations, listening to her laugh, and knowing she cared, really cared, about him. Khara had done something that no other woman had. She'd given him her heart and mind. No longer could he return to shallow relationships. He wanted more, needed more. He hadn't realized that until he'd picked Tiffany up and felt empty inside.

He wondered if Khara had any idea how

she'd turned his life upside-down. It used to be so easy for him not to become emotionally involved, to just be shallow. It had been so easy because he'd never known any other kind of relationship.

The problem with Khara was that she didn't act like his mother. He could always remain aloof with a woman who had a characteristic that reminded him of his mother — controlling, domineering. Khara acted just the opposite — sweet, kind, tender, loving, and above all, giving. He needed that. He wanted that. But in order to get it he would have to admit he was wrong. At the moment, he wasn't ready to do that. Perhaps his pride was misplaced, but that's where it would stay, for now.

Taylor rushed up to Khara and hugged her. Adam's muscles stiffened when Taylor's father, Robert Jenks, joined them. The man was a dentist with a successful practice, and was recently divorced. Everyone in town knew he was on the rebound. Adam couldn't help but notice when Robert shook Khara's hand he had held on to it several seconds longer than necessary. Jealousy surged through his veins.

On impulse he walked over to them. "Is

my mother here?" he asked Khara. He thought it sounded like a legitimate excuse.

Khara pointed to the ladies' room, then continued her conversation with Robert. "Taylor has made great progress."

"Are you here with anyone?" Robert asked. "Perhaps we could spend the day together and discuss my son's progress."

"Can I speak with you for a moment?" Adam asked and turned to Robert. "Excuse us." He gripped Khara's arm and hauled her several feet away.

She narrowed her stare at him, her green eyes flashing. "What do you want?"

"Do you know Robert Jenks just got a divorce?" Adam said in a low whisper.

"Don't you think I know Taylor's home life situation? I am his teacher. I'm well aware of his parents' divorce."

Before Adam could open his mouth to argue the point Tiffany came over and slipped her arm through his. "I've been looking all over for you. The gang has already started partying."

"I was looking for my mother," he said.

Tiffany burst out laughing. "You're kidding, right?"

Adam looked at Khara, a frown of confusion on her face. He felt the same.

"Aren't you a bit old to be spending the day with your mother?" Tiffany asked.

"There's nothing wrong with spending time with family," Khara said, sounding a bit defensive.

"Oh, come on," Tiffany said, "I mean, his mother is . . . old." She whispered the last word as if being old was a disease.

"All the more reason for Adam to spend time with her," Khara said. "He won't have her forever."

Tiffany ignored Khara and tugged on Adam's arm. "Come on, Adam." When that didn't work she rose on her toes and whispered something into his ear.

Khara walked back over to Robert and said, "I'd love to spend the day with you and Taylor. If you don't mind my aunt and her best friend joining us."

"Not at all," Robert said.

Adam watched Khara, Robert, and Taylor join his mother and Bea. He clenched his teeth and fists before he let Tiffany pull him away and back to her group. A generation gap spread between him and Tiffany and her friends. As soon as Adam spotted his friends he left her group.

"Are you ready for the tree-climbing event?" Matt Campbell asked.

Adam entered a few events every year and usually made a respectable showing. He'd been training for these events for several months but like any competition the outcome had more to do with mental attitude than physical abilities. He normally did well in the log climbing event. His strong, long legs gave him an advantage enabling him to take long strides on each step.

People came from all over the country for these competitions, many from Washington, Oregon, Idaho, and California, but also from Vermont, Connecticut and other states back East. Loggers came in all sizes and shapes and all of them had strong arms, hands, and legs. Adam had come in second in the tree-climbing competition last year and hoped to win it this year.

"I'm ready as I'll ever be. How about you?" Adam said.

Matt lifted his hands and shoulders. "You know this isn't my best event. I do better in the log-rolling event. I'm still waiting for you to enter that one."

Adam laughed and shook his head. "Sorry. Not me. I prefer land events."

Matt glanced around the area at the many people and hesitated before he said,

"I thought Khara might be with you today."

A tightening gripped Adam's gut. "She's with her aunt, my mother, and Taylor."

"Yeah, I saw the kid with his dad earlier." Matt glanced at Adam, but said nothing further about Khara or who she was with. He changed the subject by jabbing him in the arm with his elbow. "I saw you with Tiffany. She's a real babe."

Adam forced a laugh, yet he couldn't form a smile. He didn't want to be with Tiffany. He wanted to be with Khara, and suspected Matt knew that. Heck, everyone in Morton probably knew it. It was written all over his face. He'd changed since he'd met Khara. All of his buddies noticed the change. At poker night he talked about marriage, family, and children instead of hot dates, babes, and fun nights. And no one breathed a word about Khara. They'd made that mistake once and Adam had made it loud and clear that no one said one word about her that wasn't respectable.

His buddies probably thought he'd lost his mind. Maybe he had. He'd not only lost his mind but he'd lost his heart. And no matter how many days he'd spent away from Khara, no matter how many times he'd told himself she was out of his life, no matter how many sleepless nights he'd spent, he knew he couldn't live without her. The problem holding him back, holding them back was the land dispute. Until that issue got settled their relationship remained apart. Adam just didn't know how to solve the problem without one of them giving up their pride, without one of them having to compromise.

He glanced across the grounds and spotted Khara holding Taylor's hand, his father grasping Taylor's other hand. They looked like a happy family. Annoyance flared Adam's nostrils.

Matt slapped him on the back. "Come on. Let's go over to the poles and warm up."

Adam looked at his friend and noticed Matt had been looking in the same direction. Adam fell into step with Matt with neither one of them speaking a word. After several practice climbs they waited for the competition to begin. A crowd gathered to watch.

When Adam took his turn, he attached the climbing rope to his belt. Before the gun sounded he glanced into the crowd and immediately spotted Khara, holding Taylor on her lap, and Robert sitting next to her. Adam looked back to the pole and waited for the start. The second the starter gun exploded, he dug his spiked shoes into the wood of the pole and used the strength in his legs to thrust him upward. He leaned against the rope, then loosened it when he leaned forward and scaled further up. He reached the top of the pole, and didn't waste a second before he descended, which happened at rapid speed.

Halfway down the pole, Adam caught a glimpse of dark red hair. Suddenly his concentration snapped and his foot slipped. He plummeted. His head bashed against the log before he thudded to the ground. A pain shot through his arm and leg. Three men rushed forward, untied him, and carried him to a first-aid tent.

Seconds later his mother, Bea, and Khara thrust through the tent flaps. He should have known Khara would come to his aid and be there to comfort him. Whether she was mad at him or not, she was there to help him, to be there for him. He hadn't noticed the gash on the side of his forehead until she wiped it clean.

"You took a bad fall," Khara said in a soft soothing tone.

"Are you all right, son?" Dolores asked, tears of worry filling her eyes.

"I'm fine, Mom. Don't worry about me.

I've slipped before." True, he had slipped, but never from that distance. He knew it. His mother knew it. He could tell by the look in her eyes.

"You gave us quite a scare," Bea said in a shaky voice.

Tiffany burst into the tent, laughing. "You looked so hilarious. One minute you're up the tree and the next you're down." She burst out laughing.

Khara's eyes filled with anger. "He could have killed himself."

"Why don't you leave, now, Tiffany?" Dolores said. "We'll take care of Adam." She ushered the young woman out of the tent.

Tiffany shrugged as if she didn't really care one way or another, waved, then left.

Adam watched Khara as she applied a bandage to a small cut on his arm. He inhaled the clean smell of soap and the perfume she wore. His eyes traced the curve of her lips, cheeks, and nose, and the angle of her jaw. He glanced back to her eyes. "I suppose I should let you get back to Robert and Taylor."

"We're not leaving until the doctor checks you out," Khara said.

A warmth spread throughout him. How'd he get so lucky? He had three women in his life, three caring and loving women. He looked at each one of them before the doctor entered, blocking Adam's view.

After the doctor's careful examination he said, "I don't think there's any broken bones or torn ligaments or tendons. You're very lucky."

Adam sat up, bent and extended his arms and legs a few times, then stood. Minutes later Khara made her excuse to leave. All Adam could do was watch her. He wanted to run after her, beg her to stay with him, spend the day with him, and watch him in the other events. But he didn't. He couldn't.

He hobbled around the tent before he ventured outside to walk off his limp. He had yet to compete in the axe-throwing and whipsaw events. With Khara around, he wondered if he'd be able to concentrate on those events any better than he did the pole-climbing.

In the whipsaw competition, as a team, Adam and Matt made the finals. The long saw had handles at each end. The first team to cut through a log won. Adam lost in the axe-throwing event. The announcer blabbed to everyone how Adam wasn't in top form like he'd been in past years.

Adam knew why. Khara.

A long break between events gave him time to rest before the sawing competition started. As he and Matt stepped up to the log, Adam glanced over at Matt, still soaking wet from the log-rolling event. Matt had taken second, which was the best he'd ever done. He hadn't had time to change before the whipsaw event began. The power saws buzzed loudly in the background as that event continued, vibrating everything from the ground to the air.

The gun banged. The sawing roared. Quickly, Adam and Matt fell into a rhythm. The team to beat from Oregon was right next to them, the men much bigger in size than either Adam or Matt. Size didn't always determine placement. Adam had learned that from past experience.

The two teams stayed even halfway through the log. The crowd cheered them on. Adam increased their pace. They had only inches to go. To win this event would be a first for both of them. They were nearly there when, from the corner of his eye, Adam saw the other team cut through their log. He and Matt finished seconds later. They'd given it their best shot.

"I'm getting too old for this," Adam said.

Matt laughed. "Me too."

As Adam neared Khara said, "Congratulations."

His brows drew together. "I lost. I took second."

"That's a winner in my book."

Adam wanted to pull her into his arms and kiss her. Curling his fingers in his palms, he suppressed the urge. Seconds later, Tiffany joined them.

"You lost," Tiffany said, giving him her best consoling expression.

"I got second," Adam said.

"Yeah, but not first. Number one is what counts." Tiffany acted as if he'd humiliated her in front of the crowd.

Some of the men and women took this competition very seriously. They based their pride on winning or losing. Adam never looked at it as anything but friendly, fun competition. No lives would be lost over it. The Logger's Jubilee offered the people a chance to get together, see skilled loggers performing their best, and have a good time. Logging competitions had been around for centuries. Adam was proud to take part in history's tradition.

By the end of the day Adam couldn't

move. Every ache, which seemed to be many throughout his body, screamed out at him. Tiffany wanted to go to a friend's house and party. Adam just wanted to go to lie down on a soft bed, spread a jar of liniment on his body, and sleep with a heating pad. Just to move took great effort, with every muscle in his body sore. Not long ago he would have wanted to party all night. Times changed. He changed.

Reluctantly, he agreed to drive her there and stay for an hour. As he drove out of town he headed down an old country road, distancing himself from the fairgrounds, wishing he could leave his aches and pains behind as easily. Emergency lights flashed down the road on a car parked to the side of the road. As he neared, he recognized Khara's car, then her, her head underneath the open hood. He pulled up and stopped.

"What are we doing?" Tiffany said in a whiny voice. "We have a party to go to."

Adam glanced at her and shut the motor off. "I'm going to help."

"Why?"

He shut the door before she finished the word, then walked over to Khara. "Having trouble?"

Worry etched her face. "My car just died. I don't know what's wrong with it. I was just about to walk home."

Adam glanced down the road. "That's about a ten-mile walk in the dark."

"I don't have any other option."

"Now you do."

Tiffany rolled down the window and said, "Hurry up, Adam. We're missing the party."

Khara's smile faded. "Still with her, huh?"

Adam grinned. "Jealous?"

She forced a breath out. "No."

He couldn't take his eyes off of Khara. "If I help you out, what will you give me in return?" For once he felt in control of the situation and intended to make the most of it, even if that meant teasing her. His gaze dropped to her lips.

"A thank you."

"Is that all?"

"I'm afraid to ask what you have in mind." Red rose in her cheeks.

Pine resin scented the warm air; the moon rose in the sky, casting a glow upon them, and a warm breeze stirred strands of her hair. Her flushed face matched her rosy lips. Even in the moonlight the whites of her eyes contrasted with the deep green of her irises. Adam couldn't recall a time when she looked more beautiful, more alluring.

"I was thinking of a berry pie or apple strudel," he lied. It sounded like the next best thing to say.

"It's always food."

"Can't fault a guy for trying." He turned and looked underneath the hood, knowing if he gazed at her a moment longer he'd pull her into his arms and kiss her until both their heads went dizzy. "I'll get a flashlight." Within minutes he returned from his car with his toolbox. He clicked on the flashlight, then studied the engine. "I'll give you a tow home. There's not much I can do for you here." He slammed the hood of her car.

After fifteen minutes Adam had the two cars hooked up, pulled by a chain, with Khara sitting behind the wheel of her car to steer. As Adam came to a stop sign she put on the brake so she wouldn't collide into his truck. He pressed on the gas but she let off the brake late and her car lurched, throwing her forward. Adam turned around and glared at her as she braced herself with the steering wheel. He hoped his bumper would still be intact by the time they made it home.

Ten miles took forever as Tiffany didn't stop complaining even after they'd pulled into Khara's driveway. After unhooking the chain, Adam pushed Khara's car into her garage, lifted the hood and stared inside. "I told you to let me fix it for you, but you wouldn't let me," he said, an irritation in his voice, in his gut. "You said you were going to have a mechanic in town look at it."

"I forgot," Khara said.

"You forgot," Adam repeated as if she'd lost her mind.

"My car hasn't been my top priority lately."

Adam expelled a sharp breath. "I have a friend who has an old car he wants to sell. It runs well. He wants a thousand dollars for it. Can you afford that?"

Khara rubbed the back of her neck. "I don't know."

"I'll buy it and you can make payments to me," Adam said.

She opened her mouth to say something, then stopped. He suspected she wanted to refuse his offer but couldn't afford to do so. Adam wanted to give her the car. Heck, he wanted to buy her a brand-new one. Perhaps if things were different, he would.

If only things were different.

"Thank you," Khara said. She hesitated

like she was going to kiss him, then rocked back on her heels.

The door of Adam's truck slammed and Tiffany joined them. "Are we going to be here all night? Come on. I want to go."

"I shouldn't have kept you," Khara mumbled. "Thank you for your help."

"We were going to a party." Adam wasn't sure why he felt he needed to explain himself. He just did.

Tiffany glanced at Khara before a grin creased her lips. Slowly, deliberately, she rose on her toes and planted a lingering kiss on Adam's lips. "There's more where that came from, after the party." Tiffany walked back to the truck with confidence, assured that Adam would follow.

He cleared his throat before he looked back at Khara and rested his hand on the radiator. "I guess I'd better go." He couldn't keep from smiling, seeing her eyes flare with jealousy.

Without warning Khara slammed the hood of the car. Adam pulled his hand away seconds before getting squashed under the hood. "I guess you'd better," Khara said.

Darn. He didn't want to leave. They had a serious issue to resolve. He should be furious with her, and was, but he still wanted to be with her.

"You might want to hurry," Khara said. "Her parents will probably want her home by curfew."

With a chuckle, Adam walked back to his truck and got in. He met Khara's stare before he backed out and drove away.

Chapter Ten

Khara climbed underneath the sink with a wrench. The clog in her drain was at the base of the pipe's curve. If she removed that portion of the drain and cleaned it out, perhaps her sink could drain. She twisted the wrench with all her might, only budging it a fraction of an inch. She tried again, then again.

Using all her might, she groaned with effort as she loosened the pipe. Suddenly water shot out and sprayed her in the face. Khara screamed and raised her hand in defense. The water came out so fast and strong she couldn't see the pipe to tighten it up. She backed out and knelt in a growing, streaming puddle on the kitchen floor.

Instinctively she turned and looked, gasping at seeing Adam standing there, his hip leaned against the counter, laughter bubbling from his throat. "Forget to turn the water off?"

"Very funny." Water dripped from Khara's hair, face, blouse, and shorts.

Adam took the wrench from her hand, crouched down, reached in, and tightened the pipe. "There. That should do it." His sleeves were soaked.

Khara stood at the same time Adam did and muttered a thanks.

"You look like a drenched rat," Adam said followed by a chuckle. "Here, let me help you." He set the wrench on the counter and reached for a towel sitting nearby.

She took a step back as he advanced, and bumped into the counter edge. She gazed into his eyes as he wiped her cheeks and down her neck. In an unsteady voice she asked, "What are you doing here?"

He pointed to the family room. "I came to pick up more of my paperwork. I also towed my friend's car over that you bought." He dropped the keys on the counter.

Khara's glance dipped, the house dispute still a sore subject.

"You know you need someone to take care of you, to fix your clogged drains and broken down car," Adam said.

She met his gaze. "Anyone in mind?"

Adam looked away and said nothing.

Khara felt a pain pierce her heart. He didn't want her. He wanted her house and he would help her, but he didn't want *her*. That realization stabbed at her heart like an axe chopping a log in half. She swallowed and struggled to keep the lump from forming in her throat.

"I'd better get towels and clean this mess up," she said on a whisper. She stepped by him and out of the room. As she opened the linen closet where she stored her towels she took several deep breaths, but the ache in her heart wouldn't go away. She wished she wanted to lash out at him, fight him in court, hurt him any way she could because he'd hurt her. But she couldn't.

She couldn't because she loved him.

When she returned to the kitchen she found Adam under the sink dismantling the pipes. He cleaned it out, put it back together, and turned the water back on. After crawling out from under the sink, a small hole he could barely squeeze into, he turned the faucet on and watched the water drain.

"It's fixed."

Khara cleaned the water up off the floor and said, "I'm forever thanking you."

"I like you being indebted to me," Adam said. Even though he smiled he couldn't hide the sadness in his eyes, in his voice.

An awkward tension grew between them.

Khara wondered if he hurt at all because she was dying inside.

"I'll get my files and go." He didn't hesitate to leave as if he couldn't wait to get away from her.

She stepped from the kitchen before he exited the house and remained in her bedroom until she heard his car drive away.

Khara didn't want to lose her house, but fighting Adam in court wouldn't do either of them any good. Only the lawyers would win. Besides the chance of her winning was slim since he'd already taken it to court.

With a deep sigh, she wandered into the living room and sat down, depression settling over her. She had to admit to herself, if no one else, that she'd sought out a lawyer to hurt Adam because he'd hurt her. She'd reacted out of emotion, deep feelings no man had been able to touch for years.

If she had to settle with Adam being nothing more than a friend, then so be it. At least he would be in her life. He had been there for her every time, fixing the stove, repairing the house, helping her out of more trouble than she'd experienced in her entire life. And how did she show her appreciation? She'd run to a lawyer at the first chance she'd gotten.

It was her move to return the friendship. The time was now.

Khara pushed off the couch and entered the family room, the phone still sitting on Adam's desk. She picked it up and dialed the lawyer. She spent only a few minutes on the phone. That was all it took to drop the lawsuit.

As she placed the phone back in its cradle she felt as if a hundred-pound weight was lifted from her shoulders. She'd righted a wrong and it felt good.

Khara decided not to cook dinner today. The thought was a strange one for her, but what was the point? Adam wasn't there to eat it. Without him she had way too many leftovers. What she'd become accustomed to now felt strange and pointless. Every day she waited and hoped Adam would call or stop by. She knew better than to hope, but she couldn't help it.

Adam was so different from any other man she had ever known. He was kind and helpful, always ready to lend a hand, no matter the task that needed to be done. He appreciated her talents and gentle nature, which most men considered to be a weakness.

The phone rang and she stared at it. Could it be Adam?

Her hand slightly shook as she reached for the receiver. "Hello." Her voice came out breathless.

"This is Ann Turner, I'm with Memorial Hospital. Your aunt, Beatrice Thompson, has been brought here."

Khara gasped. "Oh my gosh. I'll be right there." She hung up the phone, then cursed herself for not asking what had happened. But all she could think about was getting to the hospital. She grabbed her purse, ran out the front door and jumped in her new green slug-bug, better known as a Volkswagen. The roar of the engine was deafening, but at least the car ran. In her thoughts, she thanked Adam for buying it for her. She hadn't made the first payment yet, but promised to when she got her first paycheck from the school.

As she drove to the hospital wild ideas ran through her mind. What if Aunt Bea was dying? The thought nearly stopped her heart. Bea had to be all right. Khara had become so close to her in the short time she'd lived in Morton. She couldn't bear the thought of losing Bea.

A lump formed in her throat. Her hands gripped the steering wheel so tight her knuckles turned white. A pain she'd hoped she'd never feel again pressed on her heart.

This couldn't be happening to her, not again. And this time it would be worse. She'd lose a loved one to death. At least with her parents traveling she knew she would someday see them again. Death was final and left no room, only a slow ache that took years to heal, if ever.

Tears filled Khara's eyes. There were so many things she had wanted to tell Bea, so many things she had wanted to do for her. Her tears spilled over her cheeks to the corners of her lips, the saltiness seeping into her mouth. In her mind she pictured her aunt sitting at the table, a cup of tea in front of her and a plate of freshly baked cookies in the middle of the table.

Khara realized she'd been able to talk to Bea about subjects she had never been able to talk to her own mother about, such as never marrying and living alone. Bea understood her. They were a lot alike.

She pulled into the hospital parking lot and parked in the first available spot. The second the lump in her throat subsided it grew again. Larger. She entered the hospital and hurried to the second floor. As the elevator doors opened she spotted

Adam sitting in the waiting room. Fear pierced her heart. Adam wouldn't be here unless Bea's accident was serious.

Khara rushed over to him, unable to suppress the tears from flowing. She couldn't stop herself when she threw her arms around him.

"Khara, calm down," Adam said, holding her tight.

"Is Aunt Bea . . ." She couldn't bring herself to say the word.

"What did they tell you on the phone?" Adam's brows pulled together.

She dragged in a shaky breath. "Nothing. Just that Bea was taken here."

"She'll be fine," he said in a calm voice. "She fell down a few steps and broke her leg." He pulled her back into an embrace, held her tight and stroked her hair with his hand.

All her muscles eased as the tension, the worry of thinking the worst, dissipated away. She closed her eyes and enjoyed the warmth of Adam's arms and body, her head resting against his hard chest. As if realizing what she was doing Khara's eyes widened. Awkwardly she pulled out of his embrace, suddenly feeling cold and alone, again.

"Where is Bea?" Khara asked.

"She's getting a cast put on. My mother's with her."

Khara wiped her tears with the back of her hand and had a hard time meeting his gaze. "I couldn't imagine what I'd do without her."

"I know. I've felt that way about someone lately."

She glanced at him and narrowed her stare, but refused to ask him what he meant. Her heart nearly broke on the way to the hospital today, thinking Bea might die. If he was toying with her she couldn't take two heartbreaks in one day.

"Can I get you a cup of coffee?" Adam offered.

"No, thank you. I just need to sit down." She was sure her knees would give out from relief at any moment.

Adam gestured to the couch and sat down adjacent to her, his eyes never wavering from her face that held a touch of concern.

Khara reminded herself not to read too much into his expression. Adam was a loving, giving person and would show that concern to any person in a crisis. She licked her lips, nervous about what she had to tell him. She didn't know when she would see him next and decided she might as well tell him now before he found out from her lawyer.

"I dropped the lawsuit against you. The lien has been removed from your log home. You're free to build right away." She dipped her gaze, ashamed she'd ever gone to such lengths to hurt a person that she loved so deeply.

She glanced up as Adam took her hands in his and knelt on one knee before her. "I've been thinking about our situation for days now. I think I've got the perfect solution that both of us could live with."

Khara tilted her head. "What?"

He gazed into her eyes and said, "Living with you has been the best experience of my life. I've never met a woman like you, Khara. You're loving, caring, and giving. You think of others before yourself. Do you know how rare that is?"

She didn't answer him. She couldn't. Her throat filled with that darn lump again.

"Khara Thompson, I can't live another day without you in my life. Will you marry me?"

Khara's lips parted. She hadn't expected Adam to ask her that. She tried to form a word, but couldn't find her voice.

"It's the perfect solution to our problem.

Together, we could own our land and house. There would be no land dispute between us, ever."

She cleared her throat. Trying to sound calm, despite the joy bursting from her heart, she said, "That would take care of the problem." She glanced at their hands, fingers entwined, then back to his face. "Are you sure this is what you want?"

He forced a sharp breath out. "I've never been more sure of anything in my life. I love you. Please say you'll marry me."

A cry of happiness escaped her as she threw her arms around his neck. "I love you too. Yes, I'll marry you."

Adam pulled back just far enough to kiss her. When he lifted his head he said, "I want us to be married as soon as possible." He reached into his pocket, pulled out a ring, and slipped it on her finger; the fit was perfect. "I had to guess on your ring size."

Khara stared at the biggest diamond she'd ever seen.

Dolores cleared her throat from behind them. Khara and Adam turned and looked, then Khara rushed over to Bea, sitting in a wheelchair, three-fourths of her leg in a white plaster cast.

"Are you all right?" Khara asked.

Bea patted Khara's hand. "I'll be fine. The doctor said it's not too serious."

Khara sighed in relief.

"What's that on your finger?" Dolores asked.

Khara held her hand out for both ladies to see. Adam slipped his arm around her waist. "Adam asked me to marry him. I said yes."

Bea and Dolores stared at each other for a moment before they screamed in delight. Hugs followed.

"We should have the wedding this coming weekend." Dolores rushed on with excitement saying, "I don't want to give my son a chance to back out. I've been waiting too long for this."

"No worry," Adam said, giving Khara a squeeze. "There's no chance I'd ever back out."

As Khara felt Adam's warm lips touch hers she realized that fairy tales do indeed come true.

Epilogue

Dolores sat next to Bea, still in a wheelchair, in the church as they waited for the bride to come down the aisle. They'd prepared this wedding in record time, every step pure enjoyment.

Dolores leaned over and whispered, "That was brilliant, breaking your ankle to bring Adam and Khara together."

Bea rolled her eyes. "I didn't break my ankle because of that. It was an accident."

"Whatever it was, it worked."

Dolores sat upright, but minutes later leaned over again. "Our plan to get Adam and Khara married went so smoothly that while they're on their honeymoon we'll have to plan our next scheme."

"Next scheme?" Bea asked, glancing at her friend.

"Yeah. Our baby scheme for grand-children."

Bea closed her eyes and sighed. She shook her head slightly. "*Our* baby scheme?"

Dolores jabbed Bea in the shoulder. "We make a pretty good team, don't we?"

Bea laughed. "There's that 'we' again."